Praise for *Re*

'Rich with in

this book wil. ... and readers.' – **Monica Ali, author of *Brick Lane* and *Love Marriage***

'*Reverse Engineering* will be of huge interest to both practitioners and fans of the short story and to anyone interested in how art gets made. An anthology to inspire and encourage anyone who reads it.' – **Colin Barrett, author of *Young Skins* and *Homesickness***

'This impressive collection reads like a celebration of the craft of story-writing itself. The triumph of *Reverse Engineering* is that despite accepted norms of short story craft, every author offers something different.' – **The Guardian**

'A collection of hugely illuminating conversations, packed with insights into everything from inspiration and the drafting process to setting, character, theme, ideology and the handling of voice, point of view, structure and style.' – **Times Literary Supplement**

'*Reverse Engineering* is breaking new ground for the short story, offering a unique insight not just into the mechanics of writing exceptional short fiction, but the inherent joy that is to be found in the form for both reader and writer.' – **Lunate**

'The stories in this book are excellent and varied. Knowing that the interview is waiting for us gives the reader a kind of nerdy, greedy attentiveness.' – **Review 31**

'It is a celebration of creativity itself in all its mystery, viewed through the accessible lens of short form fiction. It's such an obviously good idea, that like all such things it makes you wonder why no one's done it before.' – **Exacting Clam**

REVERSE ENGINEERING II

First published in 2022
by Scratch Books Ltd.
London

Printed and bound in Great Britain by Clays Ltd, Elcograf S.p.A.

ISBN Paperback 978-1-7398301-3-7
Ebook 978-1-7398301-2-0

Contents

Introduction

Ask a short story fan about their love of the form and you'll have to invent an emergency to get away from them. It's not our fault; we feel it needs constant championing.

It seems like there's a gap in its public perception. At Scratch Books, we made a Venn diagram of Why People Read Novels and Why People Read Short Stories – it was stark to see how little there was in the overlapping space.

From a distance, this as-yet-uncharted area can appear like a blankness. At a recent short story reading, an audience member – an author and academic – asked the panel of short story writers: 'though what *is* a short story?'

I think it was an academic question but, still, is it really so mysterious? What has got in the way of us understanding a story? Are novelists asked to account for their line of work as much?

Admittedly, it *is* difficult to talk about short stories – the great ones are such an auspicious meeting of content and form that using any words other than the story's is futile. Which means that, as we are unable to conjure it, the short story's power to haunt us is untamed... which might feel unsatisfactory, unsettling even – we are used to feeling more control than this.

Reverse Engineering II

But if there is something unknowable about the short story, maybe we can at least hypothesise about its potential, intuit something indefinite but undeniable that it must have – like a literary antimatter. The best short stories certainly have that 'there/not-there' feel to them; the way their readers receive something that the writer doesn't explicitly give.

Though the pieces in this collection are unlike each other, they are all recognisable as stories in the way they affect us. It feels that, like an edifice in time, reading casts a shadow in us. From each shadow we can understand a little about the edifice: to read a merely descriptive piece is like admiring a sculpture. But there's something about the way we participate in a story that is more like an 'inhabiting' – however mad or unlikely or unprecedented its architecture, we feel we can live in it, sensing its space from the way its characters move within it (the author, crucially, having given them the run of the place).

This interaction of living and reading is a recurring theme in the conversations in this book. As Yiyun Li says, a story's technical accomplishments and imperfections are purely the way a story aspires to live. Which is probably like how we selected the pieces for this collection – seven stories, each so vivid that it felt like life itself.

This book asks writers how they tried to create this experience. Where the first volume of *Reverse Engineering* asked writers about the choices they made, this edition asks them about writing that doesn't come from choices. The distinction is small, the difference between explaining *how* they wrote their stories, and how *they* wrote the stories.

Relatedly, when I came to edit these interviews, I found that editing out the mistakes – our cross-purposes and misunderstandings – robbed them of their vim. Which is why the interviews are presented here with all their imperfections intact.

Better than understanding what a short story is, the writers in this book give us a glimpse of what a story can be. By enquiring into the gaps and blank spaces, we pursue the unsayable within the writer, following them as they allow – and place their trust in – these vibrant absences.

Path Lights

by Tom Drury

One day, a *bottle* almost hits us. It's a brown quart bottle that falls out of the sky. We are in the arroyo, the dogs and me, walking.

They look at the bottle; they look at me. My first guess is that somebody threw it down from the rim of the arroyo. But then it would have bounced down the slope – it wouldn't have stopped dead like this.

I think of the pilot tossing a Coke bottle from a plane in the movie *The Gods Must Be Crazy*. But, as a detective once told me, 'Most of the time, we find that the thing that probably happened? Is the thing that did happen.'

So eventually I turn around and see the San Rafael Bridge – which I just walked under, so I shouldn't be surprised that it's there – and then I understand what must have happened.

Because you might not know. You might drive across the bridge and toss a bottle over the rail never guessing that people walk and ride horses below. Or you might say to yourself, 'This bottle could fall to the bottom of the arroyo and hit someone in the head, which is okay by me.'

The dogs want to get going. Either they've already forgotten the bottle or they're worried that another one might be on the way. But I tell them to stay, and I pick up the bottle and hold it in the sunlight. It's empty but still cold. Blind Street Ale is what it held.

I wonder what the dogs would have done if the bottle had knocked me out. Perhaps they would have stood by until I woke up, as Lassie would have if Jeff, or later Timmy, had been hit by a beer bottle. It's just as likely, though, that they'd have run off into the trees. Because they have their own agendas. Tag's a wire-haired Jack Russell whose life mission is to create an empire of the places where he has peed. Raleigh is a very small beagle with round golden eyes and enormous ears – homely, yet somehow profound. Her goal is to follow every odd scent she comes across – and there are, it seems, a lot of them – slowly and at length. Sometimes Tag will pee, and Raleigh will want to stop and smell *that*, and I'll think, or even say out loud, 'Well, kids, we're not going to get anywhere at this rate.'

Now we head home, where the A.C. is cranking, the blinds are down in the bedroom, and Ingrid has the blanket pulled up to her chin. She's an aerospace engineer in La Cañada and the spacecraft Phaethon has just landed on Mars. The reason for the mission is secret – she can't tell anyone what it's about, not even me.

She tends to get migraines every time some phase of her work comes to an end. I sit on the edge of the bed and put my hand on her forehead. Her hair is damp but her skin is cool.

'How was your walk?' she says, without opening her eyes.

'It was okay,' I say.

'This is the worst part,' she says. 'I think it'll break soon.'

'Do you want some Coke?'

'It's all gone.'

'Coffee?'

'Gone.'

So I run hot water on a washcloth, wring it out, and carry it back to the bedroom. I lay it on her forehead and press down.

'You're an angel,' she says.

'No, you are. Everybody else is celebrating and here you are. It's not fair.'

'I'm not worried about that, Bobby,' she says. 'I can celebrate another time.'

Path Lights

We have lived in California for three years and Ingrid likes the state very much. She was born on a farm in South Dakota. It's abandoned now. Every few years, Ingrid goes back to take a look, even though all that's left is the old bleached shell of a house, surrounded by blue grama grass and tall trees with pale bark and waxy leaves. You can't go upstairs anymore, because the steps have crumbled, but you can still stand outside and look up at her old bedroom window.

Starbucks coffee is good for Ingrid's headaches, so I head back out to buy her the biggest one they have. Then I drive to the liquor store on DeLacey and buy two litres of Coke.

'Just soda tonight?' Mr. King says.

He is short and round with a red face and bright eyes. We like him, and his liquor store. We always get him a scarf or something at Christmas, because even in Southern California you sometimes need a scarf.

'Do you carry Blind Street Ale?' I ask.

Mr. King nods. 'We hardly sell any of it, but we do have it. It's strong, and it's twelve bucks a quart.'

'Anyone buy some lately?'

'I don't know. Why?'

I tell him what happened in the arroyo.

He shakes his head and looks disappointed in humanity. 'I never heard of such a thing.'

'My idea,' I say, 'is to figure out who did it and talk to them. Not angry, necessarily, but just so they know.'

'Quite right,' Mr. King says. 'Prevent it from happening again.'

'I figure I might be able to – find them, I mean – because it's such an obscure brand.'

'I've tasted it,' he says. 'It's obscure for a reason.'

'Maybe I'll try some.'

It's dark by the time I get home. We live on a winding street with houses on one side, opposite a steep dense bank of ivy. All the houses have path lights in the grass. I really like them for some reason, these low modest lanterns lighting up when night comes down.

Tag and Raleigh are lying on the kitchen table looking out the window when I drive up. Tag stands and wags his tail so hard that the table shakes, and he yodels as he always does when he sees someone he knows outside. If he doesn't know you, his reaction is much worse. Once, a dog trainer came to the house, and he said, 'Tag is not aggressive; he's just got a tremendous amount of adrenaline.'

I take the coffee in and set it on Ingrid's night table. She's snoring lightly, but when she wakes up she'll be glad to see it, hot or cold.

Then I go back to the kitchen, open the bottle of Blind Street, and pour some into a heavy glass goblet sort of thing. There isn't much foam, which I take to mean that the bottle sat on the shelf for a long time.

The ale is flowery, with a tranquilising undercurrent. I drink it while reading the newspaper in the dining room. After two glasses, I'm sort of drunk. Gravity comes alive – I can feel it on my arms and shoulders, pulling me down.

Ingrid comes out of the bedroom now with her coffee. She sits at the table and plucks the collar of her shirt from her neck with both hands. She has straight brown hair parted in the middle and dark crescent eyes and a full lower lip that gives a strong sense of composure to her face.

'I feel better,' she says.

'Thank God,' I say.

And I mean it. I hate it when she's sick. The house gets all dark and quiet – it's as if time had ceased to function.

'Not dizzy anymore,' she says.

'Let's play cards,' I suggest.

'What are you drinking?'

I explain about the bottle and the bridge.

'I don't get it,' she says. 'You pick up some bottle off the ground and now you're drinking from it?'

'No. Hell no. I got this at Mr. King's.'

'What's it like?'

'I think you'd say it was complex.'

'Good old Mr. King,' Ingrid says.

We play three hands of Russian bank. She shuffles the cards one-handed. I don't know how she can do this, but she can.

'I could've been killed by that bottle,' I say.

'Nothing can happen to you,' she says. 'You're the voice of Milo Hahn.'

This is a reference to my work. I read out loud in a recording studio for a living. Commercials, books on tape, a few other things. Once, I even did the voice-activated response system for a tree-service conglomerate. 'Do you want *one* tree planted? Say yes or no. Do you want *more than* one tree planted? Say yes or no. Do you want *one* tree removed?' And so on. Tedious to record, let alone to hear on the phone, I'm sure. I have no doubt that voice-activated response systems are making the nation a dumber place, but the money was very good.

I also do the Milo Hahn mysteries. Milo Hahn is a private investigator who travels around the United States in a camper pickup unravelling sordid deals. That's why I talked to the detective I mentioned before – to get some background. Not that I really needed it just to read the books. The author writes three a year, and the titles are all plays on state slogans. Alaska was *Beyond Your Dreams, Within Your Nightmares*, Connecticut *Full of Deadly Surprises*.

Usually, I record at a studio in Glendale. If Martians were to land here and build their conception of an Earth city, I suspect it would look like Glendale: the open streets, the trees that line up a little too well, the eccentric and vaguely futuristic architecture.

Today I'm finishing *It Must Be Murder*, a mystery set in Maine. It concerns a woman who wants Milo to find her son. Only he's not really her son, as it turns out, but one of the world's most ingenious cocaine thieves – until, that is, his corpse washes up on a rock, where seals keep trying to shove it off, which you can understand, because it is their habitat.

'I used to be happy,' I read. This is Milo talking to himself at the end of the book. 'I'd roll into town, grill a steak, drink some Lagavulin, and watch the sun go down. Now I don't know. Now I can't chase out of my mind the crazy lies that people convince themselves of and then try to sell me. And for what? So that I'll find the answers? Make their stories true? Are you kidding me? There ain't no answers, people – that's what I want to say. No answers, no true stories. There's only the highway and a full tank of gas and a call on my cell phone from some guy in Baltimore, who's got a bit of a nasty problem and thinks maybe I can help. And the hell of it is, maybe I can.'

(The reference to Baltimore, see, will direct the audience to the next book, set in Maryland. The series goes in alphabetical order.)

I look up. Terry Finn is on the other side of the glass. He runs the sound board and lines up the jobs. He got into an accident last spring while riding his motorcycle on the Angeles Crest Highway, and had to have reconstructive surgery on his shoulder. Now he can't lift his left arm over his head.

'You nailed it, Bobby,' he says. 'Morose, yet optimistic. Only it was just maybe a little too fast.'

'Oh, you always say that,' I tell him.

'Well, you always rush the ending.'

'You know, this is in your mind. You hear what you want to hear.'

'Hey,' he says, 'I wish I did.'

This is what Milo Hahn would do about the bottle of Blind Street Ale. He would set a fire in the Dumpster at Mr. King's liquor store, and while everybody was outside trying to put it out he would rifle through the records. Milo Hahn is a master of rifling, and a combustion expert; he's constantly setting diversionary fires. When he found what he was looking for, he would rip it out of the ledger. (This is what I find troubling about the books: Milo always finds what he needs to find; in life, when you look for things, you're usually looking in the wrong place.) Later, Mr. King would probably turn up murdered, which would tip Milo off to the fact that the case was more complicated than it had at first appeared.

Path Lights

Terry says, 'Just read from the break.'

So I do.

'"Here's your money," Mrs. Cahill tells me. She's wearing an astrakhan jacket in the parking lot of an Arby's and not looking too much at home. "And a little something for your college fund."

'It's a stack of hundreds, the fresh kind, sharp as a razor, coated with the bitter powder of the vault.

'"I guess this seals the deal," I say. It's a crummy joke and I don't care if she gets it or not.

'But she does, all right. She gets it. Her eyes flash like the tail lights of a Maserati Spyder fresh off the lot, cash on the barrel, no questions asked.

'"Don't press your luck, Mr. Hahn," she says. "Someday it might press back."'

Rosemary, the herb, grows around one of the trees in our front yard, and a couple of nights later I'm cutting it back. We cook with the stuff, but you can't really cook fast enough to keep up with the growth of rosemary. The dogs are on long leads that aren't tied to anything, but they don't realise that, so they're just hanging around. The phone rings and I go inside. It's Ingrid.

'Where are you?' I ask.

'My Place.' That's what she calls Mi Piace, in Old Town. It's a big, open restaurant with white tablecloths and vast cold Martinis.

'Go ahead and eat,' she says. 'We haven't even ordered, so it'll be a couple of hours.'

'You're celebrating,' I say.

'The Phaethon has landed.'

'Another one?'

'No, the same one.'

'What's it doing?' I figure she might tell me, since she sounds a little looped.

'It's talking.'

'Oh yeah? To who?'

'I've said too much already.'

I tell her to call me when she wants to come home, and I put the phone down, though the rosemary resin on my fingers makes them stick to the receiver.

When I go back outside, Raleigh is gone. Tag lies in the grass looking melancholy. His leash is wrapped around the A.D.T. Security sign. I put him in the house and go down the street calling for our mindless little beagle. Three houses away, I see her on the high cantilevered roof of someone's garage looking down at me with big yellow eyes. Because the houses on our block are built into ledges, this is not as great an accomplishment as it seems. Still, I'm impressed.

I walk the length of the garage, and in the short distance from the front to the back the yard climbs to a bank of ground cover that's flush with the roof. Raleigh seems surprised to see me on her level when I was down on the street a minute ago.

Luckily, no one comes out of the house. I rescue my dog and carry her home under my arm like a football.

An hour later, the phone rings again. It's Mr. King this time. Four bottles of the ale I was asking about went out this morning. He heard about it but didn't see it happen. He gives me the name and address on the check.

The mission seems a little specious now, but I don't mind having something to do. So I sit down at my desk and write:

Dear Neighbours, Last Tuesday a bottle of Blind Street Ale was thrown from the San Rafael Bridge into the Arroyo Seco. As luck would have it, no harm was done. But the bottle barely missed a man and his dogs. Who can say what will happen next time? The arroyo is for the use and enjoyment of walkers and joggers and equestrians. It is almost one hundred per cent free of debris, either airborne or stationary. Let's keep it that way.

I look the letter over and change the period after the last sentence to an exclamation point.

Let's keep it that way!

It seems less hostile somehow.

Then I drive to the address Mr. King gave me, a house in a quiet neighbourhood off Linda Vista. It's one of those big Craftsman places that seem to be perpetually under renovation. Scaffolding rises on all sides, giving the house the look of a great sailing ship in drydock.

I park near the mailbox and get out of the car and put the letter halfway in the slot so that whoever lives here will see it. While I'm doing this, a deep green sports car – a Maserati, as it happens – comes around the corner and stops next to my car.

'Are you here about the environment?' the driver says. He is a man in his fifties, maybe, wearing a blue shirt with *Los Angeles Dodgers of Los Angeles* printed in white.

'No,' I say. I take the letter from the mailbox and carry it over to him. 'There was a . . . well, you can read it.'

He begins to do so and then he looks up.

'My daughter drinks this Blind Street,' he says.

Then he goes back to the letter.

'Where it says "a man and his dogs," would that be you?'

I nod. 'Probably a lot of people drink it,' I say. 'It doesn't mean she was the one.'

'One way to find out,' he says. 'She lives in the carriage house.'

'Well, you can ask her.'

'No, come along,' he says. 'She doesn't see that many people. It'll do her good.'

We drive up to the house, then get out and walk around to a split-shake barn with an apartment upstairs. The path lights here are little Mission lanterns with sea-green brass and yellow mullioned glass. Very sharp. I tell him so.

The man turns with a pragmatic flatness to his mouth, as if he had just thought of something. His eyes are deep-set, his crew cut like iron filings.

'Do I know you?' he says.

'I don't think so.'

'You seem familiar.'

'Ever listen to the Milo Hahn mysteries on audio?'

'No, I'm not familiar with those,' he says. 'I know what it is. You work for those guys – the tree people.'

'I'm the voice on their phone system. I don't really work for them.'

'No kidding. You do voices.' He nods, thinks this over. 'That can be interesting, I imagine.'

'Oh, it's like anything. Sometimes interesting, sometimes not.'

'Can you do Jimmy Stewart?'

'No. I don't do voices that way.'

'I know, I'm just kidding,' he says. 'I'm going to go see if she's around. But, whatever she says, don't get mad at her, all right? She can't stand that.'

'You know, let's forget this,' I say. 'I don't want to bother your daughter.'

'It's no bother.' He turns toward the barn and half shouts the rest. 'You've gone to the trouble to make a flyer and we're going to get to the bottom of this.'

He goes inside and is in there for some time. I walk across the lawn to a gazebo where there's an easel and a painting. The painting is dark and hard to figure out, but as I look closer I see that it must be the yard as it appears at night. The paint has been applied in thick slabs of black and midnight blue and it looks wet, as an oil painting in a museum might. I touch it – I've always wanted to do this – and I find that it is, in fact, still wet. I leave the gazebo and wipe my fingers on some ferns.

They're still in the carriage house. Raised voices bump like bats at the windows, but I can't hear anything specific. Don't get mad at her, you said so yourself, I think. I figure that Ingrid's probably calling me to come and get her by now, and here I've wandered into this weird family scene. Then the door opens.

She's older than I expected. Late twenties or more, I'd guess, in a stringy sweater with red and white stripes, over-long sleeves, and one of those collars whose points sit way out on the shoulders. Her fingers clamp the cuffs of the sweater to the palms of her hands. Her nails are short and jagged, and from the marks around them I determine that she is the night painter.

'I dreamed that God came and said it was time for me to go,' she says.

There is a wooden bench nearby with a blue-handled garden shovel leaning against the seat. The father goes over and picks up the shovel and lays it on the bench. Then he picks it up again and puts it on the grass under the bench.

'Is that how we said we'd start?' he says.

Her eyes close, press tight, and open. She chews on her thumbnail and looks at me with red-rimmed eyes the colour of slate.

'I'm sorry,' she says. 'I never thought it might hit someone. I'd had a really bad day. That doesn't excuse it, I know. See, because I dreamed that God came into my room like the mailman, and he had these orders for me in his pouch, and he said that I would die. And I said, "But I'm young," and he said, "In your heart, you are not all that young." I woke up crying, I couldn't stop, because it seemed so *real*.'

'Mariana,' the father says.

'But I don't mean to lay all that on you. Then I drove around drinking Blind Street in the sun, and I threw the bottle out when it was empty, and I drove all the way to Zuma, and walked up and down on the sand, listening to the water, and then I came back. And I felt good then, better than I had in a long time. Because I thought, You know, I'm not going anywhere. And I never thought for a minute about anyone in the arroyo.'

'Though you should have,' the father says.

'Yes. I should.'

'And?'

She rolls her eyes and breathes out so forcefully that the wings of her nostrils flare. 'And *will*, in the future.'

'Because you'll . . . what will you do?'

'Think.' She nods her head. 'I will think.'

'Look, it's not the end of the world,' I say. 'It's just a bottle. We've all thrown bottles out of cars, I'm sure, at one time or another. That doesn't make you a bad person.'

'You don't know me,' she says.

'No, that's for sure. But you're honest. You could've said, "Me? I didn't do anything." A lot of people would have said that. And that counts for something. Now, I think I've made too much of this, and I have to go.'

Mariana takes my hand in both of hers. 'My apologies again,' she says.

From their house I drive straight to Mi Piace. Ingrid and her pals are at a cluttered table in the back. I know them; they know me. There are plates and glasses and cups and saucers all mixed up on the table, and they've pushed back their chairs because the meal is over. The help hovers nearby, dressed in black.

'Where you been, man?' Ingrid says. 'I called you. Come sit by me. What's wrong? You look like you've seen the ghost of Jacob Marley.'

I pull up a chair. 'I found out who threw that bottle,' I say.

'You and that bottle, my God,' she says. 'It's like your constant companion.'

'What bottle is this?' Else Nelson, the director of the team, says.

'Oh, somebody threw a bottle at Bobby in the arroyo. It's all he thinks about.'

'Who threw it?'

'A woman,' I say.

'Why?' Else says.

I look at him. For a scientist, he looks sort of ramshackle: unshaven, jowly, with the mysterious light of extreme knowledge in his eyes.

'You tell me what you're doing on Mars,' I say, 'and I'll tell you why she threw the bottle.'

I Like Things That I Haven't Planned

Tom Drury on Path Lights

Tom Drury is an American short story writer and author of many novels, including **The End of Vandalism** *and* **Hunts in Dreams**. *His essays and short fiction have appeared in The New Yorker, Ploughshares, Harpers and Granta.*

In this interview, we spoke about the importance of vagueness in his writing process, his pursuit of what 'feels right.'

What was your initial inspiration for this story? What did you originally want to write about?

In the mid 2000s I was living in Pasadena, California, near the Arroyo Seco; I had two dogs, a Jack Russell named Scout and a beagle named Hunter. We were out walking one day when a quart bottle landed in the sand just in front of us. It wasn't a big event, of course. Something bad could've happened (the bottle hitting Scout, Hunter, or me) but didn't. It missed us. Still I wondered where such a bottle might come from and why.

I was also reading a bit of detective fiction at the time, you know, being in L.A. and everything. That was the second thread: I wanted something for the narrative voice to play against and I thought it might be fun to write passages of an imagined novel in a highly stylised detective fiction voice that was very unlike my own.

Did you already have a sense of who the character was or did he come out of that initial story set up?

I suppose the character of Bobby began as someone like me and then became his own person as I learned more about him. I can't remember why I decided to make him a voice actor, but once it occurred to me it seemed like a natural way to get to the detective fiction – the shortest distance between this story and that genre was to have him be a professional reader of it. And it just kind of went from there. (The dogs are fairly accurate representations of Scout and Hunter.)

It was a different kind of story for me because it's written in first person and present tense, and it's about the place where I was living at the time. I tend to write in third person, past tense, and the setting is usually somewhere else. My novels set in the Midwest were written on the East Coast or Los Angeles. My novel about Southern California was written in New York.

It came together very quickly, as I recall, which was unusual. Perhaps because I had a plot, which I usually don't.

Did the story change much between your first writing of it and the published version?

You know, I don't think it changed a lot. I must have revised it as I went along. But the final version which I sent to the New Yorker was more or less the way it appeared in the magazine. There were good line edits, as always, but no restructuring.

And as you revised, what changes did you make as you went?

I revised the dialogue a lot, which I always do. I also went through working on the paragraphs but, once I got to the Milo Hahn part, the structure became clear to me. Very likely I'm remembering this as simpler than it was.

Why did you add his wife's secretive job as an aerospace engineer? I wondered if this raised unfamiliar perspectives, for example, when Bobby imagines Martians' view of Glendale?

At La Cañada, north of Pasadena, we have the Jet Propulsion Laboratory – we don't have – whoever has it has it. NASA, I guess.

And I was interested in that. I've always been interested in space; I had a telescope for a while. I grew up in the Midwest, in a small town, very dark at night with big big big skies full of stars, so my interest may come from that time – being a kid, lying in the grass and looking up at the night sky.

I thought it would be a compelling line of work for Ingrid. It made sense to me that Bobby would have the voice actor job, working more or less alone in the sound booth: his pleasure in it would come from the Milo Hahn mysteries though he also does these tedious voice-activated recordings for the tree service. So his job is – I wouldn't say meaningless, but it doesn't have as much immediate significance as hers. Her job is very important, landing a secret spacecraft on Mars, so secret she can't talk to Bobby about them. Which was something I was interested in. When you have a partner, you know their work life to some extent, but really it represents another life that they have, with other people. So that became part of the story.

My favourite exchange in the story was when Bobby tells Mr. King he will talk to the culprit, to which Mr King says: 'Quite right... Prevent it from happening again.' I felt his hazy understanding and their vague conversation suggested a doomed urge to connect between them.

I wanted to ask, when you say you made changes to your dialogue, what changes did you make?

I try to make it sound more natural and to cut lines that sound unintentionally flat or don't move the story forward. I read my work aloud to hear how the conversation is working. And you're right, I think, that Bobby is trying to make a connection: with Ingrid, with Mr. King, even with those who listen to his reading of audiobooks. He wants to know who threw the bottle into the arroyo because he wants to know *someone*. But he needs a reason to pursue the whole thing, and in his dialogue with Mr. King, he finds a reason – to keep it from happening again.

I was also thinking about the way that a shopkeeper's job is basically to get their customer to the end of their conversation as quickly as they can so they can deal with the next customer. I think that's what Mr King is doing, but trying to be sympathetic as well.

Mr. King was based on a liquor store guy I knew years ago, in Providence, Rhode Island. He was a very kindly man; we would talk but there was a necessary superficiality to the conversation. I was trying to get at that and make it funny, because it's funny to me, and I also wanted the bit about this obscure brand of ale: when Mr. King suggests it's not that good, he says, 'it's obscure for a reason.'

I felt there were some clear story 'beats' with lines like Bobby's, 'Maybe I'll try some.' and Ingrid saying, 'Nothing can happen to you.' Did you work on including or excluding waymarkers in the story?

No, they happened naturally. I didn't think: *ok, I'll have him be like a detective story reader and therefore he'll make this a detective story.* It just happened in the writing. And I like things that I haven't planned. I like to find things out when I write. And that was one of the things I found out: the way the story segues from the bottle into Bobby's investigation of who threw it. As opposed to consciously creating waymarkers, I try to be open to them – to recognise them when they present themselves.

Was there a balance between how far you could use detective fiction tropes and how far your protagonist wouldn't be the perfect detective?

Well he does a good job, actually, though there's a fair amount of luck involved.

Yes, he gets very far.

I wanted a few passages of private detective language but not many, just enough to make the novel within the story a little absurd. And the whole story of a cocaine thief – I mean, I suppose there *are* cocaine thieves but it seemed to me like an unusual occupation so I was interested in that. And interested in the way things come into a story from different places – one time I was on a ferry in the Atlantic and we went by an island of rocks with seals on it, so here they are in the story.

I thought the Milo Hahn detective story illuminates Bobby's story in a variety of ways. But this wasn't something you planned?

Thinking back, I don't think it was planned. Maybe it was in my mind as something that might work or might not. Again, I wasn't trying to make him consciously mimic the actions of a private eye, but the presence of that language informs the story even though it's not Bobby's language. He's just reading it.

Which is a little bit like writing because you imagine things and you don't always know where they come from – the writer's not reading them but drawing them from *somewhere.*

And the line 'there ain't no true stories,' could be a sort of commentary on fiction or narrative in general. It's our attempt to investigate life though we don't really know the answers or how close the fiction comes to a baseline reality – whatever that might be or wherever it might exist. So here, without really trying to, I'm writing about telling stories. Which was an interesting thing to experience – I remember thinking: *ok, now this is happening.*

And was Bobby then contrasted with Milo Hahn? Where Hahn was a hard-boiled, smooth-talking investigator, Bobby is quite a garrulous overtalker, especially when he's nervous?

Yeah, definitely. The impulse was to make them different or draw a comic contrast between them. Though I think they are both a little jaded maybe. I don't know if that comes across?

Yes, though I wondered if Bobby has slightly more hope than Milo? Bobby is still looking for something while Milo only has his work?

Right, there's the line in the story to the effect that what Bobby finds troubling about the Milo Hahn mysteries is that when Milo needs to find an answer, he finds it, although Bobby feels that 'in life, when you look for things, you're usually looking in the wrong place.' It raises all kinds of questions: What is Bobby looking for? Where is he looking for it? But he is looking for something. He's not as disappointed or cynical as Milo seems to be.

It was significant to me that Ingrid can't tell Bobby what she's doing because she's contractually bound not to talk about the mission. She says the Phaethon has just landed, he asks what it's doing and she says it's talking, so I think – and this goes to the point you made about Bobby trying to connect and communicate – the dialogue between Ingrid and Bobby runs on two different levels: when she hears about the bottle, she says nothing can happen to him, he's the voice of Milo Hahn, which is kind of a way of deflecting the conversation or not really listening to what's happened to him.

With this core theme – the failure to communicate – at what stage do you add that? Does the inspiration bring it forth or is this an idea you added later?

Probably it came into the story when Bobby returns home, eager to talk about the mysterious fallen bottle, and Ingrid can't talk to him because she has a migraine, and then we get the part about the Mars mission, which she also can't talk about. Later in the story, when Bobby asks Ingrid what the spacecraft is doing, it's just a natural question for him to ask, but she says, 'It's talking,' before remembering that she's not supposed to talk about it talking. This is what I mean by things being unplanned. Talking was the most interesting thing I could think of for a Mars lander to be doing, and it was, I'm pretty sure, only after I'd written the line (and maybe some time after) that I saw how it reflected the problem in Bobby and Ingrid's relationship.

And in general I like the layer of mystery in the Mars story. I was intrigued to learn the lander was talking and wondered who it was talking to – we don't really know, we never find out. I wanted something significant to be happening on Mars. And why did I want that? I'm not really sure but it was a way to give the story of Bobby and Ingrid some complexity, because on one level this is a story about a bottle falling out of the sky which doesn't hit anyone.

We might say it's not a terribly significant thing, but I like to write about things that don't seem all that significant on the surface – events that are not dramatic or definitive but reflect undercurrents of trouble.

And this all comes together as you're writing?

Pretty much, yeah. I wanted Bobby to keep pressing, trying to find out what's happening on Mars. He doesn't really dwell on it. He just thinks: *It's a secret mission, she can't even tell me.* He doesn't express resentment or anything, but you can tell it's on his mind; I wanted him to press for the information at that moment, because of course it comes back to him at the end.

The scene when he finally confronts the bottle thrower is satisfyingly unsatisfactory – it has to do quite a number of various jobs, as well as forming a kind of denouement to his investigation. What was important in your writing of the scene?

What I liked about writing that scene was trying to capture that moment when you are trying to do something... *and then...*

Bobby's on a mission to find out about this bottle and then, when he gets to the house and the father tells him 'go ask her,' he begins to back away from his own plan. He's been doing this on a whim, really. Because he's got time to kill. But at the house he realises he might be wandering into something stranger than he'd imagined. I like those moments when the thing that you're trying to do meets with unexpected success to the point where you say: 'uh oh, maybe I shouldn't do this.'

And I wanted to get to a point where we feel how fraught Mariana's situation is. She seems emotionally troubled; she's had this dream about God coming into her room with instructions for her. That's what I mean about writing an undramatic story about Bobby on his specious mission – it leads him to something more serious when Mariana talks about the anxiety created by the dream. And what she tells him is stranger and more honest than anything he's heard throughout the story.

And I wonder if you suggest this slightly with the title? The path lights in their drive lead him to somewhere he didn't want to go...

You know that didn't occur to me until you just said it. That he didn't want to go there, I mean. That's something that's going on. There's a path created by chance events that lead him from one moment to the next and towards a bit of enlightenment in the end.

And in the story, there's a 'sharpness' to the lights. Do they have a negative quality which makes him want to back away from them?

Yes, there's a loneliness to them, the dark coming down around these little lights. There may be some connection between them and stars, though it also had to do with the path lights we had in our yard in Pasadena; the wiring in them was bad so I was constantly trying to keep them working.

So you use memories and things that are on your mind when you write?

Yeah. Another example is the little passage describing Ingrid's old house in South Dakota, this abandoned house where you can't get up the stairs because they are crumbling, but you can still look up and see the window of her room. It was a way of making a history for the character of Ingrid but it's also an abandoned house I very much remember seeing one time, just at the end of a long cornfield; I walked up to it and made a video of it; it's something I remember well so I put it in the story even though I don't really know why it's significant to me.

These connections I'm trying to make as I read, is it fair to say they are not necessarily conscious in you, the writer?

Right, they just kind of develop. Sometimes you don't see them until later. Like the up-and-down perspective in the story. The bottle comes down from the bridge and lands on the sand. The Mars lander comes down from the sky on the sands of Mars. Bobby stands on the ground and looks up at Ingrid's window. Bobby's beagle runs off and he finds her up on the roof of a neighbour's garage. There are more examples. The story has a pattern of curious or unknowable things on another level. I can see it now but it was not something I was consciously trying to do.

Although you didn't go into this level of analysis when you were writing it, how about when you were editing, when you were deciding what to keep and get rid of?

Probably more so in the editing. My questions about a given word or line or passage usually come down to: 'is it clear?', 'Does it fit?' and 'Does it sound good?' And part of what makes something like the beagle on the roof fit (to me, anyway) is the way it works as one in a series of vertical separations. They're not connected causally, it's just a pattern that runs throughout the story.

And you don't necessarily have to know what it is when you're editing but you know it's good?

I don't know about 'good.'

Well, it's not 'bad'? You don't get rid of it?

Yes. Not bad! It seems to me that it creates a kind of incidental structure in the story. For example, there's also the part where he's drinking the ale and it feels like gravity coming alive and pulling him down – it's not intentional; it probably feels right to me to make this structure, but it's not something I think about when I'm writing.

Maybe it's beyond articulation?

Yeah, I don't know, when a part of the story feels unnecessary, it is usually dialogue, or other simple things like when he says 'I'll try some,' I don't have to go on and write how he pays for the ale and leaves the shop; that can go because it's implicit, we understand that that's happening.

These are the questions I ask when I revise: *Is this sentence needed? Is this paragraph needed? Is it implicit in what becomes before or after? Is it contributing?* I don't always know *why* it's contributing, I'm not articulating or trying to create some kind of symbolic structure or anything, I'm just asking if it feels like part of the story. Maybe that sounds vague, but I try to keep it vague, relying on instinct more than analysis.

Do you think this is because you are a very experienced writer? When you were starting out do you think you had such strong instincts?

Probably not, no. You develop a way of writing, you learn more about it, and you try to become a good editor of your own work. Which is not to say it becomes easier, because for me it hasn't.

I probably wouldn't have written this story in the beginning, because in the beginning I hadn't really found a voice and a way of telling stories. And this is a story that's very much of the 2000s – it would have been different if I'd tried to write it earlier. And in any case, I would have had to wait for the bottle to fall from the bridge.

You finish the story with: '"You tell me what you're doing on Mars," I say, "and I'll tell you why she threw the bottle."' Why did you choose this as the last line?

There is an undercurrent of him wanting to know about Mars, and his resentment that he can't know. Here it seems to him that maybe he now has something to trade. He has emotional knowledge that he can trade for scientific knowledge. Now I don't believe that this trade is going to happen, nor do I think Bobby does, because the Mars team really can't discuss what they're doing, but it was an interesting question to me which was more valuable. I think the insight that he gets into Mariana's life in the backyard has value and meaning to me in a way that a mission to Mars doesn't. So I think that line is a way for Bobby to say that his world has meaning too.

I felt with that last line I understood him better, I hadn't fully *got* his resentment until then.

Me neither. I don't often end on a line of dialogue but when I found that he might say that, it felt right.

What, if anything, did you learn in the writing of his story?

That's a really good question. Probably what I learned has to do with Mariana. She's unsatisfied, living in her father's gatehouse. She has a dream that God tells her she's going to die, she's very troubled by it and then she just goes out for a drive to Zuma, walks up and down on the sand, then comes back in her convertible, drinks a bottle of Blind Street Ale and throws it over the bridge.

I have this crazy but useful idea that the characters I write about exist in some dimension, and what I'm trying to do is get their story right. Like, despite what Milo says, there *is* a true version of it somewhere.

Technically, I mean, I learned a little bit about writing a parody of a detective novel. But, really, when I look at the story, what I think about is Mariana's life.

Maintenance

by Sussie Anie

Professor Lock-up straightens behind his security screens as I push my detergent cart into the lobby. The drop in temperature shocks me. The lobby is like a refrigerator.

'Good evening.' Professor Lock-up inclines his head. 'How is The Great Dr Clean-up today?'

'I am well, thank you.'

We ask after each other's wives and children and, throughout the exchange, his gaze roams beyond me and down over his screens.

'God is good,' I say. 'Regrettably, I must hurry tonight.'

I cannot waste another minute here with him; I am no longer looking for a security man's stories, ordinary tales such as:

Professor Li has flown home already. The heat was too much for him. His ankles swelled red and he shuffled about his lab in ordinary slippers. The next week, he did not sign in at all. His replacement will come on Tuesday.

or:

You have probably heard, but Dr Huang is flying his parents out for this 'New Year' celebration they do. Imagine.

'We will talk soon.' I fish my pass from my bag. 'Another time.'

Professor Lock-up squints at his screens. His screens are divided into grids that show every empty corridor and laboratory in the

Loop's vast campus. He straightens, looks back to the glass doors and rubs his thick neck.

'I don't know if you have–'

'Oh, I have heard.'

Truly, the thrill of Professor Lock-up's ability to translate the scientists' abrupt language has faded; more so now that I am learning to understand it for myself. To hear one of their stories is to hear them all.

I no longer collect tales of decorated professors, of technicians and student researchers returning to Beijing.

I have wrung the last juice from rumours of small families and thin wives who wait indoors, afraid of how the sun might greet their skin.

These stories are everywhere. My children – even little Kofi, whose mouth is always open, who clings to his sisters' legs to stand – are no longer satisfied by them. My little ones have realised the scientists are, under their differences, like us. No children want to hear tales about people like their parents.

'I will clean Conference Suite Three tonight.' I touch my card to the reader and the glass doors part.

'We will talk soon.'

These days I seek bolder tales, of elephant ears grown on goats' backs, bearded giants hatched from gargantuan eggs, women with three pairs of eyes.

My audience grows in numbers and shrewdness each time I return; every morning the crowds that spill from my veranda are replenished with more young companions caught up in my children's games, or drawn to our home by the scent of Ohima's groundnut soup. Their eyes shine when I tell of the military trucks that rolled up from Tamale by night, and of the soldiers who escorted a herd of five-legged creatures, scaly beasts from a far off planet, in through the Loop's glass doors by moonlight.

I tell them this is why the Loop was built here, of all places, in chalky heat where sensible villagers have long ago left, where husks of houses and wells crumble to orange dust.

Maintenance

My children want news of the boys who offer their tongues to taste potions and powders, those who come by bus, missing limbs, slow to speak, men with infants' minds who limp up the road, who loan their limbs to be joined to metal claws, or to be studded with computers small as cashews.

They want to hear about the woman who sits in a room of mirrors, worrying her foamy hair, and muttering nonsense words all day. It is a spell, I tell them, and she tries again and again to make it work. She traded all she had for this spell, but it does not work at the Loop.

Cleaning Conference Hall Three will take half my shift. It is the second largest room on the campus. Well, there is a space in the basement where biological waste is stored, a chamber of discarded organic matter. Thankfully, I have no business visiting that space; it is a hall dedicated to all that is unclean, and the only maintenance such a space requires is the regular and systematic removal of waste. That chamber deep below may well be larger than any other space in here.

From outside, the Loop is a perfect ring of a building rising from flat sand-scoured plains against a skyline of pylons and a life-support web of cables. The Loop appears gently curved, but inside it is many square segments joined like links in a thick gold watch. There was a time when this story alone, of the Loop's many rooms and labs, the truth of what it was within, captivated my children.

'Tell us again,' they'd say. 'Papa, tell us about the moving stairs. Tell us about the glass floor.'

I told them with my hands: the escalator, the viewing tower where you can step out on glass sheets and see black tarmac glisten below, see how far its ingenious construction has raised you over true ground. There was a time when such stories satisfied.

I park my cart against the wall and start the disinfectant mixer. Fumes sting my throat as foam brews. I rest my foot on the shivering mixer and look up to the lights: six bowls of blue-white brilliance.

The stories I seek – composed from possibilities men like Professor Lock-up could never fathom – are clearest when electricity cuts out. I wait until lights flicker. The disinfectant mixer sputters under my sandal. I have discovered that if I start the vacuum machine while the detergent mixer runs, all the lights cut out. Sometimes, lights cut out for no reason.

Illumination blinks and dims. The mixer stills. Darkness closes around me.

I love these failures. At home we call them 'light-offs', but the scientists call them 'power shorts' or 'cuts.' In these interruptions of darkness I become, again, a man robed in white, with breath gathering hot in my mask, almost alone in Ghana's largest international biotechnology research campus. I am the one who clears crumbs of strange foods, spillages and stains, broken glass, grime from their boots and footwear, sand carried by wind or steps or smuggled in the folds of their clothes.

Tonight's light-off drags; generators are slow to respond. I reach under my shirt and pat for my beads. I wear them as a compromise for Ohima, since I insist on working ungodly hours in a place where so many sick and deformed people stay. The way she loves beads. She says before Obroni brought the Bible to our land, our ancestors ran between every force of nature with unilateral sacrifices and offerings: to wind, to sky, to fathers of fathers. Only Jesus's death made it simple.

I hold the beads and wait for tales to come.

Every morning, I return and find Settlement emptier. It was never a true village – it sprouted fifteen years ago around the bus station built to connect the Loop with routes south. I hear if you stay on the bus you can go all the way to Accra. The road reaches someway north too; families arrived from Bolgatanga and surrounding places I had never heard of, places that do not appear even when I look closely at my tablet computer's map. The map shows this place as a series of grey scabs behind the word 'Settlement.' The story behind this name is simple: when the Chinese realised workers had taken to sleeping in tents near the bus stop up to a mile along the road, they acknowledged the camp with a big sign that read Settlement. With that sign came electricians and carpenters, and plumbers who fitted flushing toilets and covered the gutters men had etched. Many of those plumbers found wives in Settlement, and remain to this day.

As the Loop grew, waves of young men came seeking work, found wives in Settlement and stayed. The Loop no longer needs bricklayers and labourers. It needs only light maintenance.

Now Settlement's strong men hover, with no business to anchor them. Men tall and healthy loiter at the bus stop in groups, in jeans and dust-bronzed vests. Chiselled unsmiling faces watch me, and fellow night-workers climb down from the bus.

Our house is visible from the roadside; it is the one that over-spills. Ohima's yellow tarp stretches back from the kitchen, and the corrugated sheets I gathered for extensions reflect the sun in white strips. Beneath the tarp wait eviscerated refrigerators, gas cookers, deconstructed motorcycles I agreed to fix.

Children rush from our veranda and their voices compete for stories, for biscuits and toffees. Older children slouch in the cool indoors, tired from sweeping the courtyard, carrying water, washing clothes, chasing chickens to flight. Little Kofi is snoring, curled with two sisters on the mat.

'Welcome, Papa.' My eldest meets me in the courtyard. He stands like Ohima: ready and eager, with curious worry in his smile. 'Please. Shall I charge your tablet?'

Ohima leans out behind him.

'Very good.' I get the tablet out and place it in his hands. Away he goes to the socket in our bedroom. The house dims as the tablet drinks power.

'You should let him use it,' Ohima says.

'Woman.'

'He could read a course. He could study.'

I explain again, my tablet computer is for work. The Loop distributed tablet computers only amongst employees.

'Learn,' they told us. 'Access our resources; try any course that interests you.'

That is how I started learning Mandarin. I listen to lessons on the bus home and on weekends, while I mend under the tarp. In addition to this, using the tablet I have mapped our route south and learned the proper process for securing visas and booking flights. In fact, I need only contact Awurama, my cousin in Kumasi, and advise her to expect us. By God's grace, after two more months at the Loop I will have saved enough to move.

First, we will move south, so the children can attend school while our visa applications progress. Later, God-willing, we shall travel abroad.

'Papa,' daughter number three tugs my trousers. Her eyes are too great for her face, big black stones. 'Will you tell us a story?'

On rare days when there have been no conferences or exhibitions at the Loop, I start cleaning anywhere I please. I usually begin on the ground floor in the first lab by the stairwell, and work up in a spiral until I reach the sixth floor's heights. There, I watch the sun rise over the plain, all of it blazing gold.

Early workers trickle in as I descend, as I check floors have dried without smears and ensure I have left no footprints. The early morning scientists are crowned with white hair. They are building big homes – in fact, whole towns – in Cape Coast, and often exchange ideas for furnishings and designs.

'It's beautiful. It is like a completely different country.'

'It was a slave port.'

'Yes. Have you visited the castle? You must.'

'Imagine how many Africans left the continent there.'

Conversation is easiest to follow when it is halting like this – when it is filled with gaps. I clear my throat, prepare to test a greeting on them.

The pause deepens so I hear gadgets ticking, feel all the Loop's strange tools pulsing, walls coursing with electricity, water gurgling through pipes and pumps, vents gasping.

I peer around the wall's curve. The scientists have hesitated, leaning close over a glistening pink ball. Whole, sitting on a tray on the white counter. A mind: like a mass of dead pink maggots. Their gloved hands touch it gently, prod it, point, as they gesture and their conversation resumes, speeds beyond comprehension.

Today, Ohima's mood meets me at the bus stop. Her anger has soured the road. I hear her chastisements as I approach the house.

'If you don't stop that nonsense,' she says, 'I will send you and this big head of yours to church.'

The children are kneeling before her on the veranda. They glance my way and bow their heads.

'Can you buy even one chicken? Do you know how to kill and prepare one?'

'No, Mama,' they chorus.

'Haven't I told you to stop worrying them? If you want to chase something, chase your own shadows.'

I sit on the step and set my bag down. Ohima sucks her teeth, stands and goes her way. Her slippers slap dust clouds.

'Papa, welcome.' My eldest rises. He wipes his palms in his shorts. 'Shall I charge the tablet?'

I pull my handkerchief out and dab my brow. 'Do you know something?'

'No, Papa.'

'The scientists at the Loop fear no gods.'

They glance up at me, all of them.

'Have you seen any of the researchers enter a church?'

'No, Papa.'

'In China, they fear no gods.'

'Why?'

I chuckle.

Their faces are wide open. Every answer waits in their eyes.

Whenever I reach the top floor before dawn, I open the cupboards where devices and gadgets are kept. The cupboards respond to command words, and opening them is a way to test my pronunciation. Scientists set odd commands for their cupboards: 'Blue socks', and 'Feed my eyes', and 'More space, please.' Tonight, I am in the prosthetics lab and the sky outside is yet to be cut by daylight. The command here is simple.

I look back. The corridor is dark, with no sign of early risers. I clear my throat.

'Dǎ kāi.' The voice sounds like it belongs to someone else. 'Dǎ kāi,' I say, higher this time.

Ohima tells me not to use my tablet outside the house, but where else will I use it? At work I must work. At home the children won't leave me in peace.

I keep it in my bag as I ride the bus, only my headphones show.

Years ago every house in Settlement was fitted with a desktop computer. The Chinese brought a very fast Internet connection here and installed one bulky computer in every home. After just four weeks, road boys arrived in vans coloured like old teeth. Waving cutlasses, they collected every computer, loaded their vans and left.

Today, the sun has risen by the time I reach home and women are washing clothes in the square. My children are still sleeping. I enter their room and watch their heaving chests.

The cost of maintaining their bodies, their little room, our sprawling home is outstanding; every month it surprises me, and compels me to work and save a little longer.

Maintenance

My children disturb each other from sleep and, one by one, fall into wakefulness. They rise and run and wash under the tarp at the back.

Ohima has breakfast ready when they return, and I announce they are invited.

While they munch bread I stir my tea. My reflection shimmers, brighter at home than when I see it at the Loop. I am luminous here. Ohima looks up at me. Her smile says she sees it too.

I look around and the children's gazes rest on me. 'I suppose you know,' I stir my tea, 'about the insects.'

'No, Papa.'

'You haven't heard?'

They shake their heads.

I set my mug down. I need both hands to tell this one. 'Whole rooms are filled with bugs in the Loop. The scientists have created mosquitos they control, with tiny cameras for eyes and speakers that cry reeeeeeeeeee. That is how they live in their land. Their politicians are always watching them.'

'Better than our own politicians,' Ohima says, and puts a plate of fried plantains before me, 'who need to be watched themselves.'

Every tool in the Loop is heavy with stories waiting to be made.

Given enough time, every story matures into truth. The truest story is of theft and decay; of returning all to dust. At the start, there was only dust. From the dust came gold, bauxite, sugar, cocoa and more. From dust came men and women with strong limbs eager to work, and work took them across oceans, to any land that would have them. Now those places fill and work grows scarce everywhere, men and women return to this dust.

But that is not for me to worry about.

Fifty thousand cedis is ten thousand euros is fifteen thousand dollars.

That is the value of a year spent worrying over the cleanliness of the Loop's floors.

'So you people don't know about the enchanted hairnets?'

'No, Papa.'

'Well. The scientists made a pair of hairnets that, when worn, bind two ordinary strangers. Any idea one has, the other person will also have. What one imagines the other person also sees.'

Silence follows.

'Will you bring one, Papa?'

'Bring one what?'

She covers her face.

'Go on. What is it?'

She peeps out at me. 'One hairnet, Papa. No, two. Two. Will you bring two so we can hear each other's thoughts?'

'Do I not bring enough?' I tickle her tummy. 'Is that not enough? Are you still hungry? Small girl like you?'

Squealing, she curls away.

Professor Lock-up says his wife is pregnant again, with twins.

'We thank God,' he says. His smile does not light his eyes.

'One sweltering day at the Loop, as scientists were going home after a hard day's work, one man – Professor Lu Chan – stayed behind. He had a secret project. He worked with animals.'

'Which animals, Papa?'

'Oh. Lizards, chickens, goats, butterflies and talking birds. Sometimes bulls and monkeys too. It is true. He was determined to restore beasts that had died and, that night, Lu Chan prepared to test his formula. What a formula. Do you know how he began mixing it?'

'No, Papa.'

'He created that formula to turn sand to forest. Yes. The scientists wanted to bring back the thick bush that once covered this land. This particular formula was too strong to use on dust, and Lu Chan was ordered to destroy it. Instead, when all had left, Lu Chan sprayed a little of the mixture onto his bald head.

'Wow, come and see. In a matter of minutes, his hair sprouted thicker than your mama's.'

'You.' Ohima, who leans in the doorway, shakes her head.

'So, that day, Lu Chan stayed late and sprayed his concoction over the still bodies of birds, goats and butterflies. He waited and watched. He waited all night. He gathered the dead animals and he tore his hair out in grief. He was so angry, he tore the animals too, tore dead birds' wings away and threw their parts in the waste chute, the chute that carries all waste to the space deep below the Loop.

'Days later, waste collectors came to empty the rubbish from that space and take it away to burn. But when the first worker entered that space, a butterfly flew out over his shoulder. He hesitated. From the basement's depths, rumbles and growls came.' I press my lips together.

'What was there, Papa?'

I lean close. 'The animal parts were returning to life, and they had become a beast of many parts. They formed a giant, made from many eyes and slices of minds and strong shoulders and claws.'

Their silence is sweet.

'And that is why only masked waste collectors in special suits enter the basement to collect waste. And you. If you don't clean your waste away, monsters may grow and stay hidden in your mess.'

Professor Lock-up says. 'Nǐ hǎo ma?'

'Wo hen hao,' I say. After that we stare at each other.

'Well said.' His posture says he has a huge story and his body is tense to deliver it.

I rummage for my pass.

'You know, we in security can see everything that is searched and read on staff tablets.'

'Yes?'

His grin is fantastic. 'My role is not just to mind security for the building; it is to make sure all our staff are safe and well.'

'Oh?'

'Well, don't I always take time to ask after your health and family business?'

'That is true. All this time I thought you were really interested in my wellbeing.'

He laughs. 'I am thoroughly interested, Dr Clean-up. That is why I love my work. We must look out for each other, you know.'

I tell him yes, I know.

'From now, let us talk in Mandarin. That way we will both improve.'

'I look forward to it.'

'We will talk soon.'

Halfway through my shift, I forget to unplug the detergent mixer before I start the vacuum. The lights beat like God himself is blinking. Darkness triumphs.

I like this darkness because when I close my eyes, nothing changes. I imagine Professor Lock-up sitting in the luminous black of his dead screens, no bigger than the body his mama birthed him with.

This morning I have an idea for a big story, a tale of computers smart enough to research without scientists. It will be a story about computers conspiring to lock patients in their rooms, and give scientists specific instructions for how every subject should be improved based on what computers deem best for them.

The bus reaches Settlement before I have thought through the ending. I take my headphones out.

Men mill around the bus stop.

Maintenance

'Good morning,' I say.

'Good morning,' they chorus.

We walk together.

More strangers wait on my veranda. Their eyes avoid mine.

Ohima is among them and stands as I approach.

'Why don't you explain?' she says. 'Explain exactly what you saw.'

One of the newcomers points at me. 'These doctors you work for. Are they really using technology to possess people?'

'Is it true they fear no god?' another asks.

I set my bag down by the step.

'We hear you have been given laptops.'

'Who said such a thing?' I say. Beyond, more crowds approach. 'Do you see any laptop here?'

A murmur of annoyance spreads.

'Don't you people have somewhere to be; is this how you mean to start your day?'

'So there is no laptop?' A youth's bare foot nudges my bag. 'Nothing is inside here?'

'Kwesi,' Ohima says. Her burning eyes say more.

I look around. I cannot guess where these men hail from. I bend and draw the tablet from my bag. They pass it around. They tap the screen, turn it over. It looks smaller in their hands.

'Anyone who works at the Loop gets one.' I clear my throat. 'You know, they are seeking more workers.'

'Work?'

'Maintaining the premises.'

'Sweeping floors?'

'The work varies.'

The man holding my tablet lifts his chin. 'Is that not your role? To clean their toilets?'

'It may well be. But that,' I gesture for my tablet. 'Is also my computer.'

Laughter is immediate, rumbling and squawking. Under the noise, my tablet is returned to Ohima, who passes it back to my eldest, who retreats into the house.

'You work there every night?' one boy asks.

'I do.'

'Is it true they are creating gadgets that will let them enter each other's heads?'

Dialogue is the zest of a story. Regrettably, none of the Loop's patients talk to me.

'Did I mention the room of skies?'

They shake their heads.

'The room is three floors high, with a ceiling of thick stone. Inside, scientists cook thick clouds and stir hurricanes. They press rain and snow from that room. They will do it here soon, you will see. They will send clouds over the dust, and raise a forest in the time a pot takes to boil.'

I am counting the money I have saved when pounding shakes the walls.

A crowd waits on my veranda, thick with road youths and lanky men in dusty t-shirts. One man removes a long knife from his pack.

'Son,' I call to my eldest. 'Bring the tablet.'

He brings it and presents it to them. It vanishes into their company.

'A simple computer,' I say. 'You can only use it for very basic things. If you want a full computer, you must be more than a simple maintenance man. They have plenty of serious computers, big tablets as well, smart phones in that place. In fact, they are still hiring.'

The tablet is returned to me.

'It is an interesting place to work. The things I have seen there.'

The quiet plunges and pulls words from me. Stories flow half-formed.

When I run out of words, they study the mat with stony eyes. They are older, it seems, than I had assumed. Bald patches spread atop their heads.

'We thought,' one says, 'they were going to open a hospital.'

'We thought they were finding ways to grow new foods.'

I shake my head.

Their eyes wait.

'Biotechnologists are not ordinary farmers, neither are they medical doctors.'

I lean closer. 'I have seen a human brain, on a table, still thinking even without a body.'

They recoil.

'A whole naked brain, pink, big like this.' I outline its shape with my hands.

'We heard they have ways to see through each other's eyes, and hear each other's thoughts.'

'Well. I saw three young women, who came from Tamale to make a little money to take them to Accra. They spoke to me, very polite young women. Well, they took part in trials and treatments. In fact, next time I saw them, they seemed different.'

It is important to take one's time with a story. To let ideas marinade and stew with silence. This is not easy; it is well known that a good story presses to be told.

'And when we spoke, I understood. Their spirits were still connected. And they said, please don't tell anyone. They wished to stay that way.' I lift my shoulders.

A youth points his knife my way and panic flares in my chest.

'The full computers,' he says.

'Yes?'

'How many do they have?'

'Plenty. I saw rooms filled with them. Of course, they are locked away. I glimpsed them on the security man's screen. If I had not–'

'Who is this security man?'
'Where does he live?'

Ohima says we must leave.

'I told you to drink with the men, stay with them. But you only talk to tell them what happens in the Loop.' Her eyes flash. 'They say you have even learned the Chinese language. Imagine. But when I say you should learn Dagbani so that you can speak with the people here you say no.'

'Woman.'

'Am I lying, Kwesi? Have I lied to you?'

'You like to talk.'

'Oh? Okay. So I like to talk. As much as you like to listen for all these stories with your big ears.'

Professor Lock-up wears a smirk tonight.

'Good evening,' I say.

'Nǐ hǎo ma?'

'Busy tonight. I have to clean Conference Room Three.'

He stands, a slow unfolding that gives me time to adjust to the shock of his grotesque height. How tapered and firm he seems. 'I expect you have heard about the One-shine machine.'

'I have not heard of such a thing.'

He dips his head. 'It is a very advanced cleaning system. It combines vacuums, mops and sprays together in one machine. The machine is intelligent; it can steer around corridors and rooms. Every floor it passes over is left spotless. In fact, floors are left so spotless you can conduct a medical experiment there on the floor and the patient will not fall ill.'

'Is that so?'

'Yes. You know, we are lucky to work here.'

'Well.'

'Do you speak Ewe?'

His Ewe is clumsier than mine, sounds fit sloppily in the shapes his words form. The meaning they carry bears the weight of fresh knowledge, though it is old news.

'When you connect too many plugs at once I can't see anything at all here. All my screens turn black.' He gestures over their displays. 'The whole building is blind and its doors will open with the meekest breeze.'

'Is that so.'

'Yes. In those moments when the power is cut, any fool can enter this place.'

A good story is one whose ending brings surprise. This ending that approaches will surprise only me, but since I am not easily surprised, it shall suffice.

Two hours into my shift, I start my detergent mixer while the vacuum is running and the resulting light-off silences both devices. Silence gives way to shouts. Thugs burst through every entrance.

As instructed, I drop my pass and run. I am just a man robed in white and I have plenty-plenty children and a wife. Returning alive to them are this character's priorities. He might be so shaken that by this incident that, upon reaching home, he will pack his family and all they own onto a bus, and head south to start again somewhere safe.

This is how the story ends: every door I push opens. I push and push into darkness and darkness turns full circle and light finds me.

Rooms without windows, deep in the bowels of the earth, are aglow. It is as though light will reclaim the Loop starting from the bottom and bleeding up. Sunrise today is indoors. A stench meets me. I know what it is, know the parts waiting to be collected. Body parts, waste and remains of beasts. The glow tugs. I fall into brilliance.

Yellow coils and tendrils tickle the shadows. Orbs of light rise in gasps.

A gaunt woman coalesces from dazzling lime, while another is birthed from clots of violet and immediately hunches and tears her foamy hair.

'So,' a voice calls. 'You were ready to leave without greeting us?'

I back away. A spiral of cold yellow tickles my cheek.

'Take us with you,' they say.

I back up until the wall slams my back.

'We won't take up space.'

'Take us.'

'We will travel inside you.'

'We won't take up space.'

I grope along the wall. When I look away, I see searing impressions where their silhouettes were.

Something soft presses my shoulder. 'Pride. Take me. I will raise you.'

'I am Hope. I will keep you.'

I bump against a slim woman whose eyes are burning coals. 'You would be a fool to leave without me. I am Wisdom.'

Wisps of steam and light reach up. The room wavers with it, with them.

'I am Guilt.'

'I don't want you. Please.'

'Don't look sad. You are not the first to see us.'

'You will not be the last.'

I push out of the room. Run.

Settlement is silent. Our house is no longer visible from the roadside. The tarp is gone from the skyline and no evidence remains of the rusting appliances and motors that sheltered there. Every house looks the same: orange walls and dull, crinkled roofs.

No children tumble out to meet me. I stop, aching, and rest my foot on the veranda step.

Ohima. She stands surrounded by packed bags, our things folded in tarp.

My eldest steps out beside her. He is carrying Kofi, whose mouth is wide open. One by one, the children emerge. Each hugs a bundle of tarp.

'Listen. I saw...' I look back. At some point the sun rose. The sky is ripe and beckoning.

'Papa.' My eldest touches my shoulder. A tarp package is strapped under his shirt; it has made him bulky where he is not. 'They have paid us. For your work.'

'I saw...'

'Papa, let us go,' my eldest says. 'There will be time for stories later.'

It's Not Just About Language

Sussie Anie on Maintenance

Sussie Anie wrote this story during her Creative Writing MA at the University of East Anglia. It went on to be shortlisted for the prestigious White Review Short Story Prize. She has since published her first novel, To Fill A Yellow House, *published by Orion in the UK.*

Written as part of her MA dissertation, 'Maintenance' was a direct consequence of her reading, her learning and her discovery of her own voice as a writer.

What was your first inspiration for 'Maintenance'? What were your early stages in coming to write this story?

It's difficult to identify the first inspiration for this story; stories often stew in my imagination for a while before I write them – it's hard to put my finger on the moment an idea becomes a thing of its own.

I wrote 'Maintenance' as part of my dissertation. I was reflecting on the role of storytelling and how it can contribute to a kind of escapism. I was also thinking about genre; I began my course at UEA very much as a speculative fiction writer, interested in future technologies and other-worldly realities – I wanted to be free from the rules of the 'real' world, to explore how the licence of the storyteller can be used to transcend realities. I wanted to explore what storytelling does to experiences of reality, and how it can be a way of reconciling reality with the supernatural or otherworldly.

I was thinking about storytelling more broadly too, as a moral tool. The character of Kwesi was central here; part of his identity as a father and storyteller involves providing moral education for his children as well as the entertainment value that his stories deliver.

In addition to all of this I was thinking about geopolitics, and investment in developing countries. I was last in Ghana in 2017 and could feel how quickly things were changing. Much of that was to do with Chinese investment, which felt like a very different interface to Western investment. Writing 'Maintenance', I was interested in stories as narratives that encompass the 'real' world but also shape it and form a retreat from it.

So themes and ideas were your starting point?

Yes, but I also wanted to have fun with the characters and the world; it was my last major piece of writing on a year out studying creative writing. I found I could use storytelling to explore themes and ideas that felt new or scary to me – I wanted to maintain that thematic approach and also have a sense of playfulness.

I loved the dignified yet ironic greeting of Professor Lock-up and Dr Clean-up. It was so subtle and touching and held the status-anxiety character flaw that later propelled the story. Was this relationship an early consideration of yours or did it come in later drafts?

This relationship became more significant in later drafts, but the importance of ego, which is revealed in this first interaction, was a key part of Kwesi's character from the start.

Again, at the time, I was thinking about the way speculative fiction can be seen a form of escapism. In that first interaction, I wanted to set Kwesi up as a character who wants his storytelling to be about something profound and transcendent, but I also wanted to indicate that storytelling becomes a way for him to claim a unique role in this frontier in the 'real' world.

There is solidarity in how the two men communicate with each other. I find, being part of the Ghanaian diaspora, nicknames are so important, a sense of seeing people from how they move through the world or by their domain or remit.

I wanted to signal the characters' roles in this space from the start, as well as the solidarity in their mutual recognition that they 'see each other' as integral to the running of the facility, a space that's new and in flux, and how that might interact with an impulse to assert authority.

Here again, it was important for the story to retain its playfulness as well as the seriousness.

I wondered if the core of your story was the tension between reality and story. How did this theme develop through your drafts? Was it important to make us as uncertain as Kwesi's audience?

This tension between different realities was a key part of the story. It was important to define what kind of physics and metaphysics the story was allowed and able to articulate, as well as what the effect of going to these spaces would be on the storyteller, while leaving room for ambiguity. In creating this sense of disorientation, the movement between the Loop and Settlement was central – seeing elements of Kwesi's home life affect his work and his work come to decide who he is at home.

It gets to the point where Kwesi's stories begin to use him and he has to chase these stories in wider circles. I wanted to question whether it's something liberating or restrictive that closes around him, considering the very real threats that exist in this world.

Did Kwesi come to you more and more as you wrote it?

I felt he had quite a strong voice from the start; I was happy to follow him through that story and through that world.

Years ago, I started storytelling thinking about scenarios that come from unusual setups and just following a constant opening of options. For this story I had a *sense* of themes I wanted to explore but I also gave myself space to follow the character. Kwesi and the setting were so clear, it was quite intuitive following him through that world.

How far did your first draft resemble the final draft?

The writing process for this story was less about having drafts and more about working out where to stop. The story's ending evolved the most through the editing process. It was very difficult to close the story down at all because it kept unfolding and unfolding and there were so many new threats that presented new questions.

Initially, I stopped at that sobering moment when the road boys confront Kwesi; storytelling had given him space to move with ease through the world but the real world had caught up with him and become present in a threatening way.

When you decided to carry on the story, what was it you wanted to add? What was the discontent with your earlier ending?

It wasn't fully realised; some of the story's themes and surrounding questions had not yet come full circle, such as what happens to the people who go into the Loop? What is Kwesi going to take away from this world? Leaving the story on that earlier cliffhanger would have missed the chance to let those themes fully manifest.

It felt too flat and too on-the-same-plane to leave it at that moment. I wanted to create a haunting feeling in the reader that maybe Kwesi's world still exists and is still unfolding – I didn't want to make the ending too neat.

The culture clash makes for great poetry in expressions such as: 'studded with computers small as cashews.' At what stage do you come to such brilliant expressions? Do they come with planning, in the first draft, or after much redrafting?

I love the harmonies that arise from juxtapositions of words and puns and double meanings, I love the playfulness of language. Some of those phrases were refined later during editing. There were a few more that I trimmed back that may have gotten in the way of the flow of the story.

I feel I'm often trying to tone down my love of language as I'm editing but here it felt intuitive because of the setting. It felt like an inherently poetic landscape where different paradigms collided and language shimmered out. I could see so many different aspects of the world folding together and where they met were wonderful resonances and harmonies. It was really fun to explore, although I had to be cautious not to make things over-written.

So your later stage was to prune these elements back? What was it that led you to cut?

There were scenes that weren't necessarily moving the story forward – I didn't want the story's movement to be impeded by beautiful language. It felt inappropriate and a bit indulgent. I didn't want the story to be just about the language itself; I wanted it to be lighter as its themes were heavy already.

Also, because previously I'd written a fair bit of fantasy with more purplish language, there was a risk of getting carried away with world-building. I wanted the world to be outlined, not too 'coloured-in.' I wanted it to feel smoky, and not like a solid dense space – some of the language I edited out was cluttering the setting.

While you were being careful to avoid your old genre styles and previous ways of telling, were you learning as you went?

Yes, I was reading a lot at the time; my MA was my first chance to really focus on literature and it felt like I was learning all the time. Because this story is very much a reflection on storytelling, I wanted to reflect openly on the decisions I was making in the writing itself.

I was thinking about the genres I was reading and what made those styles so clean and light and concise. I read Ted Chiang's stories shortly before writing 'Maintenance' – there's a resonance, a very transcendent feeling to his writing. In terms of language, one of my favourite authors is Alice Walker. I love the way she reveals characters through language so their vulnerability is conveyed in a way that is succinct and honest and poetic. That sense of an interiority that moves the story forward is something I found more in literary fiction. Toni Morrison's work blew my mind, seeing what a single sentence can achieve – how just one line can gesture towards a tension or indicate an undercurrent.

On my first reading, I was so amazed by the world in the story that I did not see the beating heart of the story: the issue of Kwesi's hopes to save money which is threatened by the road boys. Did you think in such narrative mechanics as you planned, as you wrote or was this while you edited?

It was an organic process – peeling away some of the language gave the story some of the energy that moved things forward. The structure clarified itself as I edited it; I asked myself throughout the process if the beats of the story were falling in a way that felt right.

Because Kwesi is very much absorbed in his stories, his interaction with the setting builds tension; he has his own trajectory looking for stories but the real world is slowly catching up with him. It is this tension between stories and the real world that forces some structure onto the imaginative realm that is opening up in the story.

I thought about what keeps a story moving and I think it's curiosity, that sense of journeying with someone into an unknown world. The story is about stories. It's a curiosity you are kind of aware of but able to get lost in.

When you reflected on these beats of the story, did you have to change much or find that it ticked these boxes already?

I found it ticked the boxes already for the most part, which is why writing this story was such a satisfying experience; as my narrator was a storyteller, he brought his own structure to it; he was telling stories that had their own arcs and endings and organised subparts within that story – it probably feels more organised than I made it consciously.

Was the advent of the new machine the final movement for Kwesi – the moment that now he had nothing to lose?

I wanted to challenge the stability that threatened to take over the story or make Kwesi's status seem settled. I wanted to gesture to greater stakes and deeper shifting plates beneath this world.

The nature of the Loop is kept so distant the story does not really raise it as a question explicitly, which means it becomes less a mystery the reader reads for clues and more like an empty space we are afraid to depend on. Was this consideration intentional in the writing? Or instinctive? How did you try to achieve such a subtle effect?

I wanted the setting to feel haunted – a space that's not quite there. I wanted it to feel a bit magical, like a space where anything could happen. Writing fantasy I might have reached for smoke and mists and perhaps a mystical entity that would greet and guide the reader; science fiction might focus on the experiments and the technology of that world.

I'm interested in trans-humanism and wanted to draw all its terrifying, beautiful possibilities into a setting that itself felt unsettled.

Did you get this effect the first time or have to take out things to achieve this effect?

I added more detail to the setting later. It was quite an empty space at the beginning. I liked that sense of leaving room for the reader to project and question their own expectations, a space for Kwesi to move through and alter with his stories. I wanted to integrate aspects of fantasy, science fiction, magical realism, and literary fiction, to fold genres onto genres and question the line between what's real and what's fiction – is there a line? I don't know.

I think that's where some of the poetic resonance comes from, having more technical and science fiction language alongside superstition and magical ideas, all of it grounded in a context of innovation and need. The Loop was a starting point and a place to anchor the theme of possibilities and stories.

The story seems to shift as Kwesi appears to veer into the nature of stories, leading to sentences like: 'Dialogue is the zest of a story,' and then the even more disorienting: 'Returning alive to them are this character's priorities.' What effect did you want with them? How far are we *in* Kwesi's story?

I wanted to give the sense that although Kwesi uses these stories, they grow to take over him, consuming him until he becomes a vehicle for them. I wanted to be really subtle with his disorientation – I don't know how successful I was. I could have amped that up more.

There was also a commentary on the technical aspects that storytelling relies on – that sense of being deliberate and seeing fiction-making as work. It's something I struggle with personally: I wonder what we're doing as storytellers. There are moments when Kwesi is being very deliberate and thinking, *I need some dialogue here*, so he'll be dishonest and make up things.

I also wanted to wink and say 'I'm writing a story here and it's got to have a structure and some rules.' When I started studying creative writing I was really unhappy about *studying* it because I liked the romantic aspects of being led by inspiration and not looking to follow rules; I feared that studying the mechanics of fiction would destroy the playfulness of writing.

You end with: '"Papa, let us go," my eldest says. "There will be time for stories later."' Why did you want to make this the ending?

This line was so important to me. There was a sense of being held hostage by stories and storytelling that I wanted to write about; trying to move through overlapping realities can be overwhelming. This moment at the end of the story represents the next generation taking over, suggesting we can do better, a moment that eases the burden on Kwesi. It felt important to have a note of optimism personally, as I approached the end of my MA and was about to return to the real world after having been immersed in stories for almost a year, with the hope of finding space to keep writing in the future.

What did you learn in your writing of this story?

It's difficult to keep track of. Much of what I learnt has only recently come through in the way that I write now.

One of the things I learnt was not being afraid to marry techniques from different genres, to allow things to be off-balance. I also learnt to defend my position when challenged, that I *wanted* that story to be a bit unsettled and it was okay to break some rules.

I found a voice that felt assured, in writing 'Maintenance.' Kwesi was one of the first extroverted characters I wrote. I'm introverted and it's easier for me to put that kind of personality on the page. I stepped out of my usual perspective with this story and, through that, I learned a way of immersing myself in characters very different to those I had written before.

I learned a lot about where to trim as well, and there were moments where I thought: *uh huh, that makes sense*. Before, when I had written a beautiful phrase it had been difficult to take it out, but with 'Maintenance' I learnt to be stricter about focusing on what serves the story – you don't have to make everything about language. I found that language that serves a clear purpose can help a story to breathe, letting it tell itself; writing 'Maintenance' was a very organic process and a lot of fun as a result.

Bad Dreams

by Tessa Hadley

A child woke up in the dark. She seemed to swim up into consciousness as if to a surface, which she then broke through, looking around with her eyes open. At first, the darkness was implacable. She might have arrived anywhere: all that was certain was her own self, lying on her side, her salty smell and her warmth, her knees pulled up to her skinny chest inside the cocoon of her brushed-nylon nightdress. But as she stared into the darkness familiar forms began to loom through it: the pale outline of a window, printed by the street lamp against the curtains; the horizontals on the opposite wall, which were the shelves where she and her brother kept their books and toys. Beside the window she could make out a rectangle of wool cloth tacked up; her mother had appliquéd onto it a sleigh and two horses and a driver cracking his whip, first glueing on the pieces and then outlining them with machine stitching – star shapes in blue thread for the falling snowflakes, lines of red stitching for the reins and the twisting whip. The child knew all these details by heart, though she couldn't see them in the dark. She was where she always was when she woke up: in her own bedroom, in the top bunk, her younger brother asleep in the lower one.

Her mother and father were in bed and asleep, too. The basement flat was small enough that, if they were awake, she would have heard the sewing machine or the wireless, or her father practising the trumpet or playing jazz records. She struggled to sit up out of the tightly wound nest of sheets and blankets; she was asthmatic and feared not being able to catch her breath. Cold night air struck her shoulders. It was strange to stare into the room with wide-open eyes and feel the darkness yielding only the smallest bit, as if it were pressing back against her efforts to penetrate it. Something had happened, she was sure, while she was asleep. She didn't know what it was at first, but the strong dread it had left behind didn't subside with the confusion of waking. Then she remembered that this thing had happened inside her sleep, in her dream. She had dreamed something horrible, and so plausible that it was vividly present as soon as she remembered it.

She had dreamed that she was reading her favourite book, the one she read over and over and actually had been reading earlier that night, until her mother came to turn off the light. In fact, she could feel the book's hard corner pressing into her leg now through the blankets. In the dream, she had been turning its pages as usual when, beyond the story's familiar last words, she discovered an extra section that she had never seen before, a short paragraph set on a page by itself, headed 'Epilogue.' She was an advanced reader for nine and knew about prologues and epilogues – though it didn't occur to her then that she was the author of her own dreams and must have invented this epilogue herself. It seemed so completely a found thing, alien and unanticipated, coming from outside herself, against her will.

In the real book she loved, *Swallows and Amazons*, six children spent their summers in perfect freedom, sailing dinghies on a lake, absorbed in adventures and rivalries that were half invented games and half truth, pushing across the threshold of safety into a thrilling unknown. All the details in the book had the solidity of life, though it wasn't her own life – she didn't have servants or boats or a lake or an absent father in the Navy. She had read all the other books in the series, too, and she acted out their stories with her friends at school, although they lived in a city and none of them had ever been sailing. The world of *Swallows and Amazons* existed in a dimension parallel to their own, touching it only in their games. They had a *Swallows and Amazons* club, and took turns bringing in 'grub' to eat, 'grog' and 'pemmican'; they sewed badges, and wrote notes in secret code. All of them wanted to be Nancy Blackett, the strutting pirate girl, though they would settle for Titty Walker, sensitive and watchful.

Now the child seemed to see the impersonal print of the dream epilogue, written on the darkness in front of her eyes. *John and Roger both went on to,* it began, in a business-like voice. Of course, the words weren't actually in front of her eyes, and parts of what was written were elusive when she sought them; certain sentences, though, were scored into her awareness as sharply as if she'd heard them read aloud. *Roger drowned at sea in his twenties.* Roger was the youngest of them all, the ship's boy, in whom she had only ever been mildly interested: this threw him into a terrible new prominence. *John suffered with a bad heart. The Blackett sisters . . . long illnesses. Titty, killed in an unfortunate accident.* The litany of deaths tore jaggedly into the tissue that the book had woven, making everything lopsided and hideous. The epilogue's gloating bland language, complacently regretful, seemed to relish catching her out in her dismay. Oh, didn't you know? *Susan lived to a ripe old age.* Susan was the dullest of the Swallows, tame and sensible, in charge of cooking and housekeeping. Still, the idea of her 'ripe old age' was full of horror: wasn't she just a girl, with everything ahead of her?

The child knew that the epilogue existed only in her dream, but she couldn't dispel the taint of it, clinging to her thoughts. When she was younger, she had called to her mother if she woke in the night, but something stopped her from calling out now: she didn't want to tell anyone about her dream. Once the words were said aloud, she would never be rid of them; it was better to keep them hidden. And she was afraid, anyway, that her mother wouldn't understand the awfulness of the dream if she tried to explain it: she might laugh or think it was silly. For the first time, the child felt as if she were alone in her own home – its rooms spread out about her, invisible in the night, seemed unlike their usual selves. The book touching her leg through the blankets frightened her, and she thought she might never be able to open it again. Not wanting to lie down in the place where she'd had the dream, she swung over the side rail of the bed and reached with her bare feet for the steps of the ladder – the lower bunk was a cave so dark that she couldn't make out the shape of her sleeping brother. Then she felt the carpet's gritty wool under her toes.

The children's bedroom, the bathroom, papered in big blue roses, and their parents' room were all at the front of the massive Victorian house, which was four stories tall, including this basement flat; sometimes the child was aware of the other flats above theirs, full of the furniture of other lives, pressing down on their heads. Quietly she opened her bedroom door. The doors to the kitchen and the lounge, which were at the back of the flat, stood open onto the windowless hallway; a thin blue light, falling through them, lay in rectangles on the hall carpet. She had read about moonlight, but had never taken in its reality before: it made the lampshade of Spanish wrought iron, which had always hung from a chain in the hallway, seem suddenly as barbaric as a cage or a portcullis in a castle.

Everything was tidy in the kitchen: the dishcloth had been wrung out and hung on the edge of the plastic washing-up bowl; something on a plate was wrapped in greaseproof paper; the sewing machine was put away under its cover at one end of the table. The pieces of Liberty lawn print, which her mother was cutting out for one of her ladies, were folded carefully in their paper bag to keep them clean. *Liberty lawn:* her mother named it reverently, like an incantation – though the daily business of her sewing wasn't reverent but briskly pragmatic, cutting and pinning and snipping at seams with pinking shears, running the machine with her head bent close to the work in bursts of concentration, one hand always raised to the wheel to slow it, or breaking threads quickly in the little clip behind the needle. The chatter of the sewing machine, racing and easing and halting and starting up again, was like a busy engine driving their days. There were always threads and pins scattered on the floor around where her mother was working – you had to be careful where you stepped.

In the lounge, the child paddled her toes in the hair of the white goatskin rug. Gleaming, uncanny, half reverted to its animal past, the rug yearned to the moon, which was balanced on top of the wall at the back of the paved yard. The silver frame of her parents' wedding photograph and the yellow brass of her father's trumpet – in its case with the lid open, beside the music stand – shone with the same pale light. Lifting the heavy lid of the gramophone, she breathed in the forbidden smell of the records nestled in their felt-lined compartments, then touched the pages heaped on her father's desk: his meaning, densely tangled in his black italic writing, seemed more accessible through her fingertips in the dark than it ever was in daylight, when its difficulty thwarted her. He was studying for his degree in the evenings, after teaching at school all day. She and her brother played quietly so as not to disturb him; their mother had impressed upon them the importance of his work. He was writing about a book, *Leviathan*: his ink bottle had left imprints on the desk's leather inlay, and he stored his notes on a shelf in cardboard folders, carefully labelled – the pile of folders growing ever higher. The child was struck by the melancholy of this accumulation: sometimes she felt a pang of fear for her father, as if he were exposed and vulnerable – and yet when he wasn't working he charmed her with his jokes, pretending to be poisoned when he tasted the cakes she had made, teasing her school friends until they blushed. She never feared in the same way for her mother: her mother was capable; she was the whole world.

In their absence, her parents were more distinctly present to her than usual, as individuals with their own unfathomable adult preoccupations. She was aware of their lives running backward from this moment, into a past that she could never enter. This moment, too, the one fitted around her now as inevitably and closely as a skin, would one day become the past: its details then would seem remarkable and poignant, and she would never be able to return inside them. The chairs in the lounge, formidable in the dimness, seemed drawn up as if for a spectacle, waiting more attentively than if they were filled with people: the angular recliner built of black tubular steel, with lozenges of polished wood for arms; the cone-shaped wicker basket in its round wrought-iron frame; the black-painted wooden armchair with orange cushions; and the low divan covered in striped olive-green cotton. The reality of the things in the room seemed more substantial to the child than she was herself – and she wanted in a sudden passion to break something, to disrupt this world of her home, sealed in its mysterious stillness, where her bare feet made no sound on the lino or the carpets.

On impulse, using all her strength, she pushed at the recliner from behind, tipping it over slowly until it was upside down, with its top resting on the carpet and its legs in the air, the rubber ferrules on its feet unexpectedly silly in the moonlight, like prim, tiny shoes. Then she tipped over the painted chair, so that its cushions flopped out. She pulled the wicker cone out of its frame and turned the frame over, flipped up the goatskin rug. She managed to make very little noise, just a few soft bumps and thuds; when she had finished, though, the room looked as if a hurricane had blown through it, throwing the chairs about. She was shocked by what she'd effected, but gratified, too: the after-sensation of strenuous work tingled in her legs and arms, and she was breathing fast; her whole body rejoiced in the chaos. Perhaps it would be funny when her parents saw it in the morning. At any rate, nothing – *nothing* – would ever make her tell them that she'd done it. They would never know, and that was funny, too. A private hilarity bubbled up in her, though she wouldn't give way to it; she didn't want to make a sound. At that very moment, as she surveyed her crazy handiwork, the moon sank below the top of the wall outside and the room darkened, all its solidity withdrawn.

The child's mother woke up early, in the dawn. Had her little boy called out to her? He sometimes woke in the night and had strange fits of crying, during which he didn't recognise her and screamed in her arms for his mummy. She listened, but heard nothing – yet she was as fully, promptly awake as if there had been some summons or a bell had rung. Carefully she sat up, not wanting to wake her sleeping husband, who was lying on his side, with his knees drawn up and his back to her, the bristle of his crew cut the only part of him visible above the blankets. The room was just as she had left it when she went to sleep, except that his clothes were thrown on top of hers on the chair; he had stayed up late, working on his essay. She remembered dimly that when he got into bed she had turned over, snuggling up to him, and that in her dream she had seemed to fit against the shape of him as sweetly as a nut into its shell, losing herself inside him. But now he was lost, somewhere she couldn't follow him. Sometimes in the mornings, especially if they hadn't made love the night before, she would wake to find herself beside this stranger, buried away from her miles deep, frowning in his sleep. His immobility then seemed a kind of comment, or a punishment, directed at her.

The grey light in the room was diffuse and hesitant. Even on sunny days, these rooms at the front of the flat weren't bright. She had been happy in this flat at first, in the new freedom of her married life, but now she resented the neighbours always brooding overhead and was impatient to move to a place they could have all to themselves. But that would have to wait until he finished his degree. She eased out from under the warmth of the blankets. Now that she was thoroughly awake she needed to pee before she tried to sleep again. As she got out of bed, her reflection stood up indefatigably to meet her in the gilt-framed mirror that was one of her junk-shop finds, mounted in an alcove beside the window, with a trailing philodendron trained around it. The phantom in the baby-doll nightdress was enough like Monica Vitti (everyone said she looked like Monica Vitti) to make her straighten her back in self-respect; and she was aware of yesterday's L'Air du Temps in the sleepy heat of her skin.

In the hall, she listened at the door of the children's room, which stood ajar – nothing. The lavatory was chilly: its tiny high window made it feel like a prison cell, but a blackbird sang liquidly outside in the yard. On the way back to bed, she looked into the kitchen, where everything was as she'd left it – he hadn't even made his cocoa or eaten the sandwich she'd put out for him, before he came to bed. His refraining made her tense her jaw, as if he had repudiated her and preferred his work. She should have been a painter, she thought in a flash of anger, not a housewife and a dressmaker. But at art college she'd been overawed by the fine-arts students, who were mostly experienced grown men, newly returned from doing their national service in India and Malaya. Still, her orderly kitchen reassured her: the scene of her daily activity, poised and quiescent now, awaiting the morning, when she'd pick it up again with renewed energy. Perhaps he'd like bacon for his breakfast – she had saved up her housekeeping to buy him some. His mother had cooked bacon for him every morning.

When she glanced into the lounge, her shock at the sight of the chairs thrown about was as extreme as a hand clapped over her mouth from behind. The violence was worse because it was frozen in silence – had lain in wait, gloating, while she suspected nothing. Someone had broken in. She was too afraid in the first moments to call out to her husband. She waited in the doorway, holding her breath, for the movement that would give the intruder away; it was awful to think that a few minutes ago she had gone unprotected all the way down the lonely passageway to the lavatory. Then, as her panic subsided, she took in the odd specificity of the chaos. Only the chairs were overturned, at the centre of the room; nothing else had been touched, nothing pulled off the shelves and thrown on the floor, nothing smashed. The lounge windows were tightly closed – just as the back door had surely been closed in the kitchen. Nothing had been taken. Had it? The wireless was intact on its shelf. Rousing out of her stupor, she crossed to the desk and opened the drawer where her husband kept his band earnings. The money was safe: three pound ten in notes and some loose change, along with his pipe and pipe cleaners and dirty tobacco pouch, the smell of which stayed on her fingers when she closed the drawer.

Instead of waking her husband, she tried the window catches, then went around checking the other rooms of the flat. The kitchen door and the front door were both securely bolted, and no one could have climbed in through the tiny window in the lavatory. Soundless on her bare feet, she entered the children's bedroom and stood listening to their breathing. Her little boy stirred in his sleep but didn't cry; her daughter was spread-eagled awkwardly amid the menagerie of her stuffed toys and dolls. Their window, too, was fastened shut. There was no intruder in the flat, and only one explanation for the crazy scene in the front room: her imagination danced with affront and dismay. Chilled, she returned to stand staring in the lounge. Her husband was moody, and she'd always known that he had anger buried in him. But he'd never done anything like this before – nothing so naked and outrageous. She supposed he must have got frustrated with his studies before he came to bed. Or was the disorder a derisory message meant for her, because he despised her homemaking, her domestication of the free life he'd once had? Perhaps the mess was even supposed to be some kind of brutal joke. She couldn't imagine how she had slept through the outburst.

This time, for once, she was clearly in the right, wasn't she? He had been childish, giving way to his frustration – as if she didn't feel fed up sometimes. And he criticised her for her bad temper! He had such high standards for everyone else! From now on, she would hold on to this new insight into him, no matter how reasonable he seemed. Her disdain hurt her, like a bruise to the chest; she was more used to admiring him. But it was also exhilarating: she seemed to see the future with great clarity, looking forward through a long tunnel of antagonism, in which her husband was her enemy. This awful truth appeared to be something she had always known, though in the past it had been clouded in uncertainty and now she saw it starkly. Calmly and quietly she picked up each chair, put back the cushions, which had tumbled onto the carpet, straightened the goatskin rug. The room looked as serene as if nothing had ever happened in it. The joke of its serenity erupted inside her like bubbles of soundless laughter. Nothing – *nothing* – would ever make her acknowledge what he'd done, or the message he'd left for her, although when he saw the room restored to its rightful order, he would know that she knew. She would wait for him to be the first to acknowledge in words the passage of this silent violence between them.

In the bedroom, she lay down beside her husband with her back turned; her awareness of her situation seemed pure and brilliant, and she expected to lie awake, burning at his nearness. There was less than an hour to wait before she had to get up again; she'd got back into bed only because her feet were cold and it was too early to switch on the electric fire in the kitchen. But almost at once she dropped into a deep sleep – particularly blissful, as if she were falling down through syrupy darkness, her limbs unbound and bathing in warmth. When she woke again – this time her little boy really was calling out to her – she remembered immediately what had happened in the night, but she also felt refreshed and blessed.

A young wife fried bacon for her husband: the smell of it filled the flat. Her son was eating cereal at the table. Her husband was preoccupied, packing exercise books into his worn briefcase, opening the drawer in his desk where he kept his pipe and tobacco, dropping these into the pocket of his tweed jacket. But he came at some point to stand behind his wife at the stove and put his arms around her, nuzzling her neck, kissing her behind her ear, and she leaned back into his kiss, as she always did, tilting her head to give herself to him.

When the bacon was ready, she served it up on a plate with fried bread and a tomato and poured his tea, then went to find out why their daughter was dawdling in the bedroom. The girl was sitting on the edge of her brother's bunk, trying to pull on her knee-length socks with one hand while she held a book open in front of her eyes with the other. Her thin freckled face was nothing like her mother's. One white sock was twisted around her leg with its dirty heel sticking out at the front, and the book was surely the same one she had already read several times. The child was insistent, though, that she needed to start reading it all over again, from the beginning. Her mother took the book away and chivvied her along.

Always Slightly Betraying Life

Tessa Hadley on Bad Dreams

Tessa Hadley is the author of eight highly-acclaimed novels and three short story collections. In 2016, she was awarded the Windham Campbell Prize and the Hawthornden Prize. In 2018, she won the Edge Hill Prize for Bad Dreams and Other Stories, *which included this story.*

In this interview, we spoke about creating fiction from personal memories and writing 'straight through, slowly.'

You've said in another interview ['This Week in Fiction: Tessa Hadley,' The New Yorker website, Sept 2013] that the girl's dream and vandalism were both childhood experiences of yours, although they took place at separate times for you. Why did you decide to fictionalise these real life experiences?

As a short story writer, I'm always in search of stories because it's the story, the actual matter of it – *what happened* – that's the hardest thing. It's getting the story that's the challenge. And then, once you've got your initial premise, that's not enough by itself. It's the fulfilling of the promise of the premise, taxing and exacting as it is, that's sort of delicious.

And because you need quite a lot of short stories – you only need one good novel idea every couple of years – you're always on the lookout for a good story. Sometimes you have a time when they're really coming at you thick and fast and sometimes you have a slightly barren stretch. So you're pushing for material in anecdotes, in what you read – that could be fiction or non-fiction, or in your own experience.

I've never forgotten the dream I had, in real life, about *Swallows and Amazons.* And that 'not forgetting' is interesting in itself, as I'm usually terribly doubting about memory. I have a mum who is wonderful but very inflexible with her memories; she is so certain she can remember how things were and, as a reaction, I'm so uncertain. I think we make most of it up.

But I *knew* I'd had this dream, and I've never forgotten it, which means that I must have gone on retelling it to myself over the years, since I was seven or eight. I remember too – as far as anyone can be sure a memory is authentic – that one line from the dream: 'Susan lived to a ripe old age,' which horrified me and chilled me. I'd always kept that piece of memory, although I hadn't prodded at it as a story before and I've no idea why suddenly one day it seemed full of potential.

And I'd always had this funnier, lighter memory, which is a family story of me at the same age, turning all the furniture over one night in the living room while my parents were having a dinner party and were in the kitchen eating and laughing. I'd felt shut out from their fun and made this disruptive gesture of turning the chairs over. And for years, my mum did think it was one of the men at the party. She looked at him quizzically, waiting for him to confess, not just that night but a long time afterwards, until I mentioned it years later and all became clear.

Somewhere – and these adhesive moments are lovely, when the first premise and another piece of story come together – these two fragments must have suddenly grown together, and I must have felt vividly at the same time how exciting it would be to go back inside that very flat where it all happened. I'm often skirting close to autobiography in my writing, but not usually quite as close as in this. But even those two elements – the dream and turning the furniture over – didn't quite add up to a whole. Getting the fact that the mother would wake up and find what the child had done, that was what delivered the whole story. And then I suspect that the very last piece, the final section, arrived while I was writing all that, discovering I needed something else, a third thing, to tie them together to finish it.

So you started out not knowing the destination?

Yes. I knew that it hinged on a misunderstanding, which is a very good piece of fictional structure; it's always rich because you can have your story two different ways. You can have one person thinking or doing things this way, and the other person coming in and not getting it, seeing everything differently. And that's a generative structure if you like. But I didn't yet have the neat throwaway gesture at the end.

I was really impressed by the rhythm and timing with which this opening unfurled. What stages did you go through to get the effects you wanted for the girl's dream epilogue?

I am a pretty dense slow writer and I'm not a rewriter. I will have put the sentences down pretty much in the order they are in now. I know I began at the beginning: those first sentences feel like a beginning, when the child 'seemed to swim up into consciousness as if to a surface, which she then broke through.' And of course that's what the story does as you begin to read it; as its reader, you're kind of rising into the story and looking around you.

So I always just write straight through slowly, and I can't move forward until I feel a given paragraph or section is right, and is done. I will have done some rewriting but that will have been local edits and nothing structural. The three pieces of the story and their proportions didn't change.

Getting the rhythm and timing is hard, but it can't be arrived at by calculation. You have to feel it sensuously, so you might as well do it first time through. You've got to feel your way to timing, and part of that is, whenever you sit down to write, reading your work over and over again and trying to feel it not as the writer going a sentence at a time but as the reader, thinking: *I'm bored now, that's too long spent there, now I need to move on.* So you come to feel the rhythm of the writing as you write, rather than coming back to it later.

Although of course, especially with a novel, you do have a day when you read again the section you wrote three months ago and you think: *that's too long* or, *there's a piece missing,* and then you can go back in structurally. That sometimes happens with a short story when you see you've gone down a rabbit hole there and need to come back out. But I'm pretty sure that with this story and a few others I more or less got it first time.

You say you only moved on when you felt you had it right, is it impossible to articulate what that feeling is?

Probably yes, there's no going beyond that. There's a brilliant bit of Wittgenstein – he always seems brilliant to me, though mostly in ways I don't understand; yet there are sections in *Philosophical Investigations* that any writer can appreciate. There's a wonderful paragraph where he says the *smell* of the word has to be right, to fit what we mean to say. And though he says *smell,* I often think about the eye.

Writers can get quite sentimental about the sound of the words. Of course sound matters – I love reading out loud to an audience, but I don't ever read what I'm writing out loud to myself. It's for the eye: I'm *looking* at it over and over again until my brain is tired, trying to get the flow through. You're breaking up that sentence and then pulling back from this one, and reshaping that paragraph – all for the eye. Is this the truthful right version or is it not? Although, how does one test for truth in a sentence...? Somehow you have a scene in your mind's eye, you are testing and correcting against that scene. It's like a painter looking at the subject, looking at the canvas, making a mark and then looking back at the subject and then back at the canvas, correcting the mark. That seems a very good analogy for what it feels like.

Reading your stories in general, I get the sense of you 'watching' a character, then using what you've seen to understand the character's inner life. Is this in any way close to how you write your characters?

Isn't it funny that we are discussing vision again? For instance, I'm always worrying about the lighting, always trying to think: *what will she be able to see? What will the thickness of this darkness be like? How can she see the back of the flat as the moonlight comes in?*

So, yes, I am *seeing* it. Although we also have that thing going on that only prose fiction can do – drama can't do it, and films can't do it, marvellously visual as they are – which is that the writing moves seamlessly and fluently back and forward between watching the little girl moving in the flat, and feeling her experience from inside her. Fiction can give the whole contents of her awareness, which we can't see from the outside.

I loved putting that word 'Leviathan' in there incidentally, which is borrowed from life. My dad did an external degree in economics and one of the things I remember about this as an eight-year-old was that he had Hobbes' *Leviathan* on his shelf, though I wouldn't have known then what it was, I only remembered that name. I don't know if I had any sense that Leviathan was a whale: but it spoke to me of something important, and I loved putting that word there on the page, with all its spreading resonance. Anyway, that's the miracle of prose fiction, that movement back and forwards between watching the child from outside, and being inside her mind. Of course a great filmmaker and dramatist can achieve something like that, but they have to work harder to contrive it. That movement is so at ease inside this kind of writing.

I saw the word 'Leviathan' as an extension of the 'massive' Victorian house, and another part of the enormity of the world up against her vulnerability.

Yes! Though I can't say I consciously thought about that. It's like our earlier question, 'how do you know when it's right?' You put down a word like 'Leviathan' and you feel it resonating forward and backward through your text. It's so delicious when a word strikes a rich note like that; it's one of the ways you know you're getting somewhere truthful, when the tuning fork rings and all the other things in the previous pages ring too.

The minute anyone invokes a house in fiction, it makes me think of Jung; although I'm not a Jungian and have never read any Jung. But this is my cod version of Jung: that he uses a big house with all its storeys as a suggestive image for representing human culture; the cellar full of primeval mysteries, the attic with its sophisticated elite art. The family in my story, anyway, is in the basement of that massive Victorian house, as indeed we were – and it was pretty massive to a little girl. And feeling all those lives on top of your head, as my child does, is a way of expressing how a child comes into the world and has all this superstructure of culture and society to learn to grapple with.

And that's not me asking: *how can I cleverly express the weight of coming into the human world.* It's rather me thinking: *here she is in the basement flat of that great house and it feels like...* The movement is that way round, from the material ordinary reality with all its vibrations *into* the layers of meaning. Which I think is mostly how symbolism works in fiction. Not *I will cleverly sew in a sequence of moon images*. It's not like that, you start with a real moon rising on a real night, then the moon sets off its resonance around the prose.

You've said you knew before writing that the story would include the mother's response to the daughter's actions, what did you want this section to add to the story?

I did know, because I wouldn't have embarked on writing it if I'd only had the little girl's part. It is a 'two hands clapping' story. It was only when I'd got the (completely invented) idea of the mother finding what the child's done, and misinterpreting it, that I knew I had a story to write.

In fiction there's so much space for misinterpretation. Which sounds a negative thing – it *is* a negative thing, in life. It's frightening, perhaps, that we misread each other so much, even as we manage to rub along together. But that potential for misinterpretation allows something lovely inside a story – an openness, avoiding final judgement. You can hold in your story these two contradictory versions of what happened: unreconciled, not sorted out, there they sit beside each other on the page, aesthetically bonded together. It's something generous that fiction does that individual subjectivities can't easily do: sustaining, side by side, two different contradictory versions of what happened. This transcends the solipsism of individuality. That's making it sound complicated, but it's actually what every reader likes, I think, in fiction. They like a book full of different people, who don't all agree.

Though mostly absent in the hours of this story, we sense that the man, the father, is usually the more influential agent in the family. In the descriptions you give of him, why did you choose these details?

There's a simple answer which is; they *were* my dad. *Leviathan*, the external degree, the relative absence – he was often out, at work or playing in his jazz band – the trumpet, the jazz music that he would have been playing if he had been awake. That's one of the ways the little girl knows the adults are asleep: there is no music. Those were the signs of masculinity that were littered around in my flat when I was a little girl; they're good signs, they stand usefully for a male preoccupation. There's the intellectual life, the abstraction of books embodied in *The Leviathan* and in those files full of papers.

I just reread that bit where I said that the child fears for her father's vulnerability. I don't know where that came from – well, I do know. My dad died a couple of years ago. I thought of him as a very strong man, such a powerful, potent man; but I was always anxious that he would fall somehow. That's funny, isn't it? Even as a child I was aware of some vulnerability in him. As if there's a risk in that strong assertive masculinity, which exists somewhat outside the home. The risk isn't there in the mother, the little girl doesn't fear for her mother. She feels that her mother is strong, is *in* her world, has it all under her control; while her father is risking something, by going out away from the home.

The trumpet, the books, the intellectual endeavour, the father's absence: these all suggest a fairly old-fashioned patriarchal family, in which the mother is on guard at the hearth, keeping the home values burning. As we learn in her section, there is some fairly significant, ancient feeling of conflict with her husband's masculinity. That ancient antagonism was what I wanted to get at in the story: not just, *oh dear, they don't really get on, do they?*

The quite frightening vision the woman has, of some lifelong antagonism, it's sort of the ancient sex war. It's her being a woman and his being a man, and when she thinks he's thrown the furniture, she imagines on his part some violent refusal of her domesticating, taming female activities, a refusal that she is going to have to live with and yet not yield to. As well as touching on this ancient sex antagonism, this was also a portrait of my family. Although I'm not sure that my mum would own up to my vision of this antagonism being an element in their relationship, I think there was some truth in it.

And even though it wasn't him who tipped the chairs over, is there some degree that the realisation she comes to is a true one, that she has an insight there?

Yes, it has to be, otherwise it's just an awful story in which a near accident gives rise to an awful mistake.

Conrad's novel *Chance* is built around two people who really love each other but completely misunderstand each other's feelings, and so for a long time can't be together. That's interesting in itself. But in this story I want the reader to feel that although this young wife misinterprets the facts, she's actually found something important which has some reality in it. It also suggests how we stumble around blindly in relation to each other – even in a marriage, especially in a marriage – because we can't wholly know the other person. Very often there *is* an inbuilt antagonism in a marriage, however loving the bond is.

So yes, you are meant to feel more than just *oh no, what a disaster, an awful mistake has set them on the wrong track.* That's another reason for needing that third brief part at the end: it's to reassure the reader that life is going to go on as usual. They will all forget, or half forget, what happened that night, and that's all right. And yet under the surface of 'all right' there is all this churning engine of interpretation and misinterpretation, and relationships made in the dark.

I felt that last act as a premature closing of the issues in the story, as if I'd been ejected out of the world before I could get to an assurance that the characters would be ok.

It feels like a long shot in a film, as if we've come out of the story and we're looking at it now from a long way away, and without sound.

And there I suppose I'm partly being personal. I'm drawing away from the story, which had seemed so close to my own life. No story *is* your life, after all. It's always slightly artificial and slightly not you. It did feel very poignant to imagine that family and that flat, and yet it is all made up and it isn't exactly what my family was. So that's another interesting aspect of any story: that you're always aiming at the heart of life, and hungry to capture life, but you're always just slightly betraying it and making it up, falsifying it, slipping off to one side. That's got to be acknowledged in the prose as well somewhere.

In the previous interview you describe a 'double-facedness' to the story: the characters both change and continue, both have revelations and misunderstand, both suffer losses and are restored. Were these nuances something that you discovered as you wrote as opposed to something you altered afterwards, as you edited?

Editing is normally about rhythm and length and so on. But it's not about *putting in* nuance; the nuance has to be there from the beginning, in the matter, in the core of the story. And built into the very structure of this story is that twin element: those two pieces that fit together like mirror images but are also very different. That synchronicity between the two stories isn't something that you could edit in afterwards.

I found your last sentence so tender and raw: 'Her mother took her book away from her, and chivvied her along.' Why did you decide to make this your closing point?

When I reread it just now, what I really liked was the description of the girl: 'trying to pull on her knee-length socks with one hand while she held a book open in front of her eyes with the other... One white sock was twisted around her leg with its dirty heel sticking out at the front.' Those are the kinds of sentences that writers are most delighted to have achieved. One of my favourite things in all writing is a line from Joyce's 'The Dead.' It's freezing outside as the guests arrive at the musical party, and the buttons of Gabriel's overcoat when he's undoing it make 'a squeaking noise through the snow-stiffened frieze.' And you just know that feeling and that sound of the button in the frozen cloth. That's the best joy that writers get. I so remember pulling on those horrible nylon socks we used to wear in the Sixties which, after a few washes, went hard and became really difficult to pull up your leg. Then they would fall down, if you didn't wear elastic garters. I was so pleased to get that dirty heel in words, twisted the wrong way.

I can just imagine this child starting again with *Swallows and Amazons*, because this final part is all about starting again. The night before, both the girl and the mother have been at some extremity. But what's wonderful about mornings is, you fry the bacon, your husband kisses your neck, you start the book again, everything recommences. We are slightly inside the mother's perspective in these closing moments of the story, though only just, only fragilely. When it says 'The child was insistent,' we're watching the mother almost as much as we're watching the child through her eyes. 'The child was insistent though, that she needed to start reading it all over again, from the beginning.' We know why the child's insistent, her mother doesn't know.

I think *thank goodness for ordinary life.* It's fine. She'll get back to the book. She'll be reading it again in two minutes. Once her mother's made her pull her socks up and put her shoes on, she'll be back inside it. Then she'll be off to school and back at it again after school that afternoon. She's going to make it all right again, she's going to bring those dead Swallows and Amazons back to life.

What, if anything, did you learn about writing in your work on this story? This is a very personal moment that you are laying out in front of us.

I think it was exciting to write this story because it was so nakedly personal. In the middle of the story I describe that moment where the little girl is standing in the sitting room: 'She was aware of their lives running backward from this moment, into a past that she could never enter. This moment, too, the one fitted around her now as inevitably and closely as a skin, would one day become the past: its details then would seem remarkable and poignant, and she would never be able to return inside them.'

Of course, as I wrote that, and was that very child, grown into an adult, the details of that scene did seem precisely that: remarkable and poignant. And I would never be able to return inside them. The story is essentially situated from an adult perspective. It fits with something that's a preoccupation of mine – and of everyone, of course; that is, the conundrum of *presentness.* The present as we feel it in a given moment feels fitted so tightly around us, it's so whole and so unanswerable. And then it turns to nothing behind us. Where does it go?

I have been back – much more recently than writing this story – to that house in Bristol. I stood on the drive of this great house which had seemed so grand to me once, and which had become so sordid and shabby. The flat where we once lived was sad, I wasn't even sure if anyone was living there. I was aware of having written this story and aware of having lived in that place and

I thought, *what was that present? Is this the same place now that it once was?*

I'm sure you know that wonderful children's book, *Tom's Midnight Garden* by Philippa Pearce, from the 1950s. I would say it was my seminal reading because it was for me the first book that grappled with this elusiveness of present and past. When Tom goes back into the garden and into the past, and makes friends with Hattie, gradually the reader becomes aware that the young girl Hattie *is also* the grumpy old lady who lives upstairs in the house in the present. And that is such a destabilising, brilliant conceit.

I think that mystery of present and past is foundational in my imagination really. I did feel, writing those sentences about the little girl aware of existing in her present, which won't last forever, as if I came to some centre there. I remember feeling powerful, because I could put down into a story something so deep and important and truthful to me. So it was a good story to write.

Ancient Ties of Karma

by Ben Okri

It was a clear bright day and there were these two men who were about to have a duel. One had a long knife and the other had a short sword that curved sharply at the end. The one with the knife was younger, cockier, and a little wild. He was very sure of himself. The one with the longer weapon was older, more civilised, and did not want the fight, and did everything to avoid it. But the younger one forced the situation, and they had the first of their fights.

It began in a flash. One made a move, the other ducked, and suddenly the younger one plunged the knife in the older man's chest. But this was in a shadow realm. Then both of them, who must have been friends, travelled on. They walked through many landscapes, and traversed many cities. Then outside a railway station they had another flash fight. The one moved, the other ducked, and the younger one planted the knife in the other's chest. But this was in a realm of thought.

The two men, bound together by mysterious ties, journeyed on. All the travelling together had not resolved the enigma of the bad blood or the fated mood between them. Then the day of doom arrived. Fate had given them time to overcome, and they hadn't. The older one never provoked, but was bound to the younger one by ancient ties of karma. They came to a village in the woods. It was near a cemetery. They were now in real time.

The younger one provoked. Then a shadow flashed between them. The younger attacked, the other ducked, and stuck his weapon somewhat desultorily at the younger one, who made an evasive movement and then, for real, planted his long knife deep into the belly of the older man. But the younger one, not satisfied with victory, was outraged at the poor technique of the older fellow. So while he still stood conscious, with the knife sticking out of him, the younger one decided to give the older man a lesson.

He replayed their moves. The older one had made a thrust; he, the younger, had moved sideways and extended his left arm so the knife went harmlessly between arm and body; and then he had delivered the coup de grace. He was almost triumphant.

But then the older one suddenly came to life, and made these extra-ordinarily swift movements, faster than the shadow of the wind, faster than thought. The older man made three slashing cuts and brought the sharp curved end of his weapon down on both sides of the younger one's neck, but without touching him.

It was a series of master strokes. It was evident, suddenly, that the older one could have killed the younger man easily, whenever he chose. It was evident that the older one was a master all along. He had deliberately refrained from killing or hurting the younger one.

Then something bizarre transpired. Suddenly, in his awareness, all that was true in the shadow world happened and the younger man fell as if he had been fatally struck. He fell against the wall and as he sank to the ground, he cried:

'Hell has opened for me. He has come for me.'

And right next to him the wall flowered into the yellow brightness of a monkey's head which projected in reds and yellows from the wall, engulfing and encompassing the younger man as he screamed out the inaudible wail of Don Giovanni being dragged down to the underworld.

While this happened the older man sat beside him, silently swept up to heaven, accompanied by the harmonious melodies of the sirens.

A Disruption of the Conventional

Ben Okri on Ancient Ties of Karma

Ben Okri is a novelist, short story writer, poet, playwright, and essayist from Nigeria. He is author of more than eighteen books and has received such literary prizes as the Commonwealth Writers Prize and the Booker Prize for Fiction.

In our interview, I wanted to know more about the choices he had made to come to such a dream-like piece.

What was your first inspiration for this piece? Why did you want to write this stoku?

You did not ask the key question. What is a stoku? A stoku is an amalgam of the short story and the haiku. It follows the other conditions of the haiku except the 17 syllable and three-line requirement. This means that it is always a work of brevity. It has one fundamental difference from the traditional short story: it follows dream-logic. It is not a dream, but is structured like one. It was a form I developed between 2007 and 2012. *The Comic Destiny*, a volume of stokus, shows the manifold configurations they can take.

The inspiration for this stoku was numinous. I wanted to explore the realms through which an unknown past affects the present, as well as an ancient aesthetics of self-cultivation whereby those who know are silent and those who don't are expressive.

Ben Okri

This story feels a product of a spontaneous, unconscious following of inspiration. What work – honings, parings and other changes – did you do in subsequent drafts?

It was much shaped. The spontaneous feeling you get is an illusion produced by the chosen mode of writing. I was guided by the truth of the sentences.

Many writers are taught to evoke the reader's imagination by showing not telling. However, with expressions like: 'But this was in a shadow realm,' what were the benefits of telling instead of showing here?

The telling/showing dichotomy is a false one. 'It was the best of times and the worst of times…' 'It is a truth universally acknowledged that…' 'Happy families are alike…' I could go on. Sometimes showing is telling, and telling is a higher form of showing. To tell is, at best, to distil. Sometimes telling saves dozens of pages. Think of how many pages it would have taken Dickens to show us that it was the best of times and the worst of times. Also, from a purely linguistic point of view, one tells a story. We have to be careful about mantras that become laws. Writing is a fluid and complex art. Properly used, 'telling' contextualises and is efficient. It is one of the tools of brevity.

With some of your expressions, the reader is asked to make leaps they may not be used to in 'conventional' genres of story. Did these 'distant stepping stones' come evenly to you or did you have to work on this method? Did you feel a need to guide the reader in *how* to read this story?

The story, the tone, guides the reader in how to read it. Good stories make up the secret laws by which they are read. All stories are strange. That's why they are stories. Every line in a story has to be earned. Fought for and earned.

And yet, at other times, the narrator uses more conventional signposting to foreshadow oncoming drama. How did you calibrate the balance of the conventional with the unique?

Every story calibrates the conventional and the unique in accordance with how much the story conforms to the comfortable and accepted mode. My stoku is a disruption of the conventional. The two tinctures are mixed carefully, so you are both unbalanced and reassured.

The story appears to obey the rules of folklore that the younger's bad behaviour will be punished. Is there wise counsel or a community warning in the story?

What you call the folkloric element is just the way the mood moves from the ungraspable to the tangible. No counsel or warning is intended. Just a melodic line following its own contours.

This stoku uses oral techniques in places, as if it is being spoken to us. I wondered if it was intended to create the illusion of a physically present narrator, or was it more a wish to return from our modern solitudes to something like live communication and its sense of community?

I am not aware of using techniques of orality. I just wanted to tell a story of these two people who are fatally bound to one another for reasons they can't fathom.

At times the narrator's colloquial style can seem spontaneous and maybe even 'artless', in other places there is a very orchestrated and literary building of effects. How much was this story the product of a controlling authorial intent and how much were you 'gifted' the story involuntarily?

All good stories are intended, even when inspired. You have to earn everything. It is harder than one thinks to make something seem 'artless.' Stokus are shaped. The dream-logic is deliberate. What you feel as a reader is a product of art.

What did you want this ending to do?

To have the effect of music.

What, if anything, did you learn in your writing of 'Ancient Ties of Karma'?

I'm always learning.

All Will Be Well

by Yiyun Li

Once upon a time, I was addicted to a salon. I never called ahead, and rarely had to wait – not everyone went to Lily's for a haircut. The old men Lily called uncles sat at a card table, reading newspapers and magazines in Chinese and Vietnamese. The television above the counter was tuned to a channel based in Riverside, and the aunties – related or not related to the uncles – watched cooking shows and teledramas in Mandarin.

I was the only customer under sixty, and the only one who spoke in English. With others Lily used Vietnamese, Cantonese, or Mandarin. The first time we met, I lied and said that I had been adopted by a couple from Holland when I was a year old and that we moved to America when I was in middle school. Lily forgave me then for not being able to speak one of the languages she preferred. Brought up by foreign devils, she told a nearby auntie in Cantonese. Half foreign, the auntie said; hair still Chinese. Half devil, Lily said; brain not Chinese. Both laughed. I smiled blankly at Lily in the mirror, and she smiled back. What do you do? she asked, and I lied again and said I was a student. She picked up a strand of hair and let it fall. My hair had just begun to show signs of grey. What subject? she asked, and I said I'd gone back to school because I wanted to become a writer. Will you make money being a writer? she asked, and I said not really.

Lily's salon was a few blocks from the high street where armed robberies rarely made even the local news. The salon was caged in metal bars, and there was a chain on the door, which Lily unlocked when she saw her customers coming and locked again right after they entered. If there was a fire, none of us would escape, I had thought when I first started to go there, though that didn't alarm me. I had two small children then, both in preschool, but, despite others' warnings, I did not feel susceptible to the various dangers that the world could dole out. If the world had a mind to harm, it would do so to the prepared and the unprepared equally. Does being a mother give one the right to bluff? If having children is a gamble, one has no choice but to bluff.

We lived on the college campus where I was teaching at the time. Enclosed within the fences was a land of trees and ponds and creeks and fountains. The flowering quinces near our house were said to have been planted by the servants of the founder's family in the eighteen-sixties. The preschool was in a building that, with its white stucco and Spanish tiled roof, looked like an outdated resort in the Mediterranean. America was a young country, California among its youngest states. The college was a mere débutante in a world of grand, old institutes, but all those trees and bushes and buildings gave me the impression that life could be as slowly lived, as long-lasting, as we wanted it to be.

Still, the world was full of perils. Some rather real, some rather close. Once, campus security sent out a warning that an unaccompanied pit bull had been spotted roaming near the swimming pool. Once, an armed man was chased into the cluster of faculty houses on a Saturday night; with police cars and helicopters outside, we turned off our lights and listened to a CD of a French children's drama called 'Madame Magic,' designed as a language course. Sometimes a drive-by shooting happened on the street corner near the preschool, and on those days the children were deprived of their outdoor time. All these threats, strangely, didn't worry me as much as the eucalyptus trees. A recurring fear I had, during those years, was that on a windy day a eucalyptus branch would fall on our heads. In one of the earliest conversations about nature I had with my children, I pointed out that the settlers had made a mistake introducing eucalyptus trees to California. A fire hazard in the dry season, I said, and in winter storms there was the danger of falling limbs. That didn't scare them, though; on our walks they would sing, 'Kookaburra Sits in the Old Gum Tree.' Someday, we decided, we would go to Australia and see koala bears and kangaroos and kookaburras.

When I went to Lily's, I wore a dark sweatshirt and blue jeans, with a twenty-dollar bill tucked in the back pocket. Once, returning to campus after a haircut, I ran into a colleague. My goodness, she said, I thought you were a student. I blend in, I replied. I could easily have booked an appointment at a boutique salon in one of the more picturesque suburbs. Lily's was only a few blocks from the college, but was my time so precious that I couldn't drive twenty minutes to a safer neighbourhood? Mencius said that a man of wisdom does not stand next to a wall that is about to topple. Even though I wore sneakers and was a fast runner, I should have known that nobody can outrun a bullet.

I went to Lily's more often than was necessary. Had I been superstitious, I would have thought that she had put a spell on me.

Lily liked to chat. There were always dramas in her life. Once, her husband broke a toe when he tripped on the carpet that they had finally installed in their house, after ten years of planning. Once, her youngest son, who went to a state university, overslept on the very same morning that a man hacked at random pedestrians with a knife on their street. 'He could've been killed,' Lily said. 'He's the laziest of the three, but now he says it pays to be lazy.' Her father-in-law, just before his death, had made friends with a man whose first name was Casino. 'The poor man thought it was a sign that he would win some money,' she said. 'Turned out Casino was not a true friend. Casino didn't even go gambling with him.'

I listened, smiled, and asked questions – these were my most tiresome traits, and I used them tirelessly. Each encounter was a test I set up for myself: How long could I get people to talk about themselves without remembering to ask me a question? I had no stories to share. I had opinions, and yet I was as stubborn as Bartleby. I would prefer not to, I would reply if asked to remark on people's stories. In any case, Lily didn't care about my opinions or my stories – she got plenty of both from the uncles and aunties. I liked to believe that she had waited years for a perfect client like me.

Elsewhere, I wasn't entirely free from the demands of stating my opinions. Once, a student complained about a J. M. Coetzee novel I'd assigned. It's so insulting that this book is all about ideas and offers nothing for the heart, she said, and I snapped, unprofessionally, that in my view bad taste was more insulting. Once, a student called Charles Simic a misogynist because he hadn't written enough about his mother in his memoir. Read a book for what it is, I admonished the student, not for what you want it to be. The student replied that I had only stale ideas of what literature was about. 'My goal is to dismantle your canon,' she said, pointing to the Tolstoy and Chekhov on my desk. 'They're not about real life.'

What is life? I wanted to ask. What is real? But right away I felt exhausted. I longed to sit in Lily's chair. She would trim my hair and talk about the bubble-tea-and-frozen-yoghurt place her husband had decided to invest in, or her neighbour's new profession as a breeder of rare goldfish, or her oldest son's ridiculous dream of quitting his job at the law firm and attending a culinary institute. Canons did not have a place in Lily's life. If she were to dismantle anything, it would be a house worth buying as a flipper.

So I went to Lily's. To my surprise, that day she did not want to talk about her husband or children or in-laws. Or perhaps it was a different day when she decided to tell me a love story. It didn't matter. All those stories she had told me before had been only a prologue.

It took one haircut for me to get the bare bones of the story, and a few more to gather the details, and still a few more for me to start looking at Lily askance. What was real? What was life? Perhaps we could all make up stories for ourselves when we didn't know the answers.

All Will Be Well

Here's Lily's story.

She grew up in an ethnic-Chinese family in Vietnam. At sixteen, she fell in love with the Vietnamese boy next door, who was sixteen, too. She was beautiful, he was handsome, but when war broke out between their countries the following year Lily's father decided that it was no longer safe for his family to live in Vietnam.

'Tuan came to my parents,' Lily said. 'He asked to leave the country with us. He would do anything just to be with me, he told my parents. My father said, "You're not our son, you're your parents' son."'

I thought about that war, three weeks and six days long, which was nearly forgotten now. When I was in elementary school in Beijing, my best friend subscribed to a children's magazine that often featured stories set on the border between Vietnam and China, with illustrations of maimed bodies and bombed villages and the heroic faces of intrepid soldiers. But, placed in history, that war was no more than a skinned knee or a sneeze to mankind. When Lily asked me if I knew the history between the two countries, I almost slipped and said yes. Then I remembered: I was supposed to have grown up in a country far from Asia, with an enviable childhood.

Lily's family had become boat people, migrating from Vietnam to Hong Kong to Hawaii and later to California. She had helped her parents in their Chinese takeout, apprenticed with an older cousin who ran a hair salon in Los Angeles, married, and had children. This nondescript life of an immigrant would have continued, if she hadn't recently had news of Tuan, the boy of her girlhood.

'Our story is like a movie,' she said.

'Like a play,' I said. 'Romeo and Juliet.'

'Do you know someone who can make our story into a movie?'

For a while, Lily kept asking me that, and each time I replied no, feeling bad for delivering disappointing news, yet not bad enough to stop going to see her. Years of standing in the same spot – cutting and shaving and dyeing and listening to the uncles and aunties – had turned Lily into an unhurried storyteller. She took detours, and, like a verbal magician, offered dazzling distractions and commonplace tricks. 'Where does your husband get his hair cut?' she asked once. 'Tell him to come here. I'll give him a discount because you're my best client.'

More people came into the story, marching in and out like a platoon of extras. Her schoolmates were remembered. Some of them had also had crushes on Tuan. The friendships between the fathers and between the eldest sons of the two families were recollected, but friendships severed by war were hardly worth a movie. Lily's parents had sympathised with their daughter when they first left Vietnam, but soon afterward they had shown impatience when she pined.

'Well, I can't blame them,' Lily said. 'Love doesn't put rice in the cooker or a roof over our heads.'

'What does love do?' I asked.

'Oh, love makes a good movie,' she said. 'Without movies, what would we do with ourselves?'

Tuan cried for three days and three nights in front of Lily's old house after she and her family left. No one could pry his fingers off the chain lock. At the end of the third night, his older brothers were finally able to take him back to their house. Everyone thought he was going to die.

'Three days and three nights,' Lily said. 'Never a step away from our door.' She had heard about this from an old friend whom she had seen recently when he and his wife were visiting their children in America.

Could anyone cry non-stop for three days and three nights without food or drink or sleep? But what right did I have to doubt the boy, what right did I have to want him to express his heartbreak more poetically or die more realistically, like Michael Furey? For all I knew, Michael Furey had been a figment of Joyce's imagination, as perhaps the boy was of Lily's. I did not know sorrow then, and later, when I did, after my elder son's death, I thought that Lily's young lover had been fortunate to have so many tears in him. Sorrow only desiccated me. Tears came to an end. Desiccation persisted.

The boy did not die. He recovered and eventually moved to another province in Vietnam to teach mathematics at a middle school. A woman in town fell in love with him, though he did not reciprocate. 'He was waiting for me to come back,' Lily said. 'Before we parted, he said he would wait for me all his life.'

A life of waiting was interrupted by a bout of illness, during which the woman took care of Tuan like a good wife. After that, the two were married, and together they raised three daughters.

'Isn't it interesting that he has three daughters and I have three sons?' Lily said. 'Think of where our promises went.'

'Did you promise to return?' I asked.

'Of course I did, but we left as refugees. We knew we wouldn't go back.'

'But he could've kept his promise.'

'Now, that'd be a really good love story,' Lily said. 'But I don't hold it against him that he didn't. He shouldn't have.'

The next time I went to Lily's – after I'd been away for two months for the summer holidays – she looked ruffled. 'Where have you been all these weeks?' she asked, and before I could answer she said, 'My friends have put me in touch with Tuan.'

'Did you see him?'

'No. How can I? We aren't the kind of people who take time off from work, and he lives in Vietnam,' Lily said. 'But they gave my contact information to him. He wrote and asked about my family, and told me a few things about his wife and daughters.'

Everything was fine, then, I thought. A love story had arrived at a tranquil ending.

'He asked me to forgive him,' Lily said.

Oh dear, I thought.

'Do you think I should call him? He asked me if I would be willing to talk on the phone.'

'Why not?' I said.

'What if I turn out to be a disappointment? Not the girl he remembered?'

'It's only a phone call. You won't see each other. You'll just hear each other's voice. Say a few nice things. You don't have to talk about the past. The two countries were to blame, not the two of you.'

'What if he turns out to be different from the boy I remember?' she said.

'Maybe you shouldn't call him, then,' I said. 'You don't have to.'

'But how can I not? If I miss him this time, we'll miss each other all our lives.'

The phone call didn't go the way I had imagined. I had thought that Lily and her former lover would have a bittersweet conversation about their youth, and exchange a few superficial details about their marriages and their children, nothing too concrete, happiness and adversity both withheld. Or that they might be more forthright as adults and take a philosophical view, agreeing that their love might not have weathered the changes as they grew older. They would tell each other that they would remain friends. They might even say that their two families could become friends.

But I'm not a good writer of love stories. There are more things in Heaven and Earth than are dreamt of by my limited imagination.

When Lily finally called, the man had no words but only tears, and she listened to him sob. 'He was disturbed,' Lily told me. 'I almost felt like crying myself, but I kept saying to him, "Hello, do you have something to say? We've waited for this for so many years. We can't waste our time crying."'

After a long while, as he was still crying, one of his daughters took the phone away from him. 'It's too much for Father,' she said to Lily, calling her Auntie. Lily asked the girl about their family life in Vietnam, and she answered with warmth. 'Father often talks about you,' the girl said. 'We all feel you're part of our family.'

Lily was working on the nape of my neck when she said this. I couldn't catch her eyes in the mirror. She didn't sound perturbed when she recounted the girl's words, which troubled me. Her voice was dreamy in a menacing way, like a voice-over in a movie. I pictured an actress standing in front of an open window, her back to an unlit room, the moonlight cold in her theatrical eyes. Does he deserve your love, or does he deserve to be killed by you? she asked herself, her face frozen with indecision. Do you have a choice?

'And then,' Lily said, 'you won't believe this. The daughter said that all three sisters' names have a Chinese character from my name. I never told you. My Chinese name has the character 'blossom' in it. He put the same character in their names.'

I shuddered, the way one shudders when stepping out of the hot summer sun and into an abandoned tunnel. Where had that thought of a tunnel come from? And then I remembered. It was an abandoned nuclear shelter next to our apartment building in Beijing. My parents' generation had dug the tunnels when it was feared that a war between China and the Soviet Union was inevitable. In elementary school, I had played truant often and gone into one of the tunnels with a box of matches. The damp and mouldy air, the scurrying bugs and rats, the rusty nails I had collected in a box as treasure – I felt terror imagining my children on an exploration like that. Yet I had been happy then.

'And then his daughter said, "Auntie, I don't think Father can talk with you today. It's too much for him. We worry about his health. But do you want to talk to Mother? She is here. She wants to talk with you, too."'

'Did you talk to his wife?' I asked, knowing that Lily's pause was a gesture to allow me to be included in her narrative.

She did. I would have, too.

'Do you know anyone who could make this into a movie? I'm telling you, it's a love story, and it's a movie.'

'I don't know anyone who makes movies,' I said. 'But what happened? You talked with his wife, and then what?'

'She came on the phone, and I liked her voice right away. I think he married a good woman. She called me Sister. Like the daughter, she also said he talked about me often. And then she said, "You don't know how much he loves you. You will never understand." And all of a sudden I started to cry. Imagine that. I didn't shed a single tear when he was bawling on the phone. His wife said, "But you shouldn't cry, Sister. You should be happy. You're the only love he's had. All these years he's kept your photo on our nightstand."'

'In the bedroom the two of them share?' I asked.

'Yes,' Lily said.

'Are you serious?'

'Why would I lie?'

Why would anyone lie to anyone? But people do, I thought, all the time.

'I talked with his wife and then with the two other daughters,' Lily said. 'It was a long phone call. And I didn't hear a single word from him. But you know what made me the saddest? His wife said, "You're the most beautiful woman I've ever known." No one has ever said that to me.'

We both looked up at the mirror. I had not thought of Lily as a pretty woman. I was an exhausted young mother then, courageously blind to the dangers of the world and stubbornly blind to its beauties. I now studied Lily, and thought that she was indeed pretty. I also started to think that she'd made up the whole story, just as I had invented my upbringing in Holland. We all had our reasons for doing this as long as no harm was done. Even so, I began to resent Lily. She must have put a spell on me, tricking me into her chair, hypnotising me with girlish dreams that had not been hardened by life.

'Maybe you can write my story, and then someone will make a movie from it,' Lily said.

I should have stopped going to Lily's right away. Perhaps she had seen through me. Tell me a story – she must have known that every time I sat down in her chair I was making that request – a real story, Lily.

Let me tell you a story – she agreed – and let me make it unreal for you.

We saw each other one more time after that. She had promised to show me a copy of the photo of her and the boy, the one he kept in his marriage bedroom. A photo would prove nothing, I thought, but where else could I go for a haircut? Finding another salon would be like starting a new relationship, forging a new friendship, while all I wanted was to keep the unknown, good or bad, at a distance. Forget life, real or unreal. What I wanted to do was to raise my children as a good mother should. In those years, the days seemed long, never-ending, and sometimes I felt impatient for my children to grow up, and then felt guilty for my impatience.

The photo that Lily showed me – what can I say? Years later, after my son died, I felt a constant ache, similar to what I had felt for Lily and the boy when I saw them in the photo. The same ache, I imagined, would afflict those who now looked at photos of my son – he died at about the age Lily and Tuan were when they fell in love.

But that ache was still as distant and as theoretical as a nebula when I was sitting in Lily's chair. She opened an envelope in which a sepia-toned black-and-white photo was preserved between two sheets of tissue paper. The girl in the photo was dressed in a white áo dài, and the boy in a white silk shirt and a pair of white pants. She was beautiful, he was handsome, but those were not the words I would use to describe them. They were young, their faces cloudless, their bodies insubstantial, closer to childhood than to adulthood. They looked like two lambs, impeccably prepared by their elders as sacrifices to appease a beast or a god. Would anyone have been surprised to hear that they died right after the photo was taken? Some children were born tragedies.

'What do you think?' Lily asked, studying my face.

'Wow,' I said.

'Maybe you can write a romantic novel about us.'

When tragedies drag on, do they become comedies instead, or grow more tragic?

I could not make a romance out of Lily's story. She was not the first person I had let down with my writing. During those years, when my children were in preschool, at the beginning of each semester we were asked to send a care package that was to be kept at the school in case of a catastrophic earthquake. In the care packages we were to include a few non-perishable snacks, a family photo, a small stuffed animal, and a note to the children, telling them that, if their parents could not make it to the school, there was nothing for them to worry about. Everything would be fine, the note was to say. Everything would be all right in the end.

I had always prepared the snacks and the stuffed animal and the family photo, but I had never been able to write that note to my children. What could I say to them? If your teacher is reading this to you, it means that Mommy and Daddy are late picking you up; it may also mean that we will never come back for you, but all will be well in the end.

We lived through their childhoods without being hit by a deadly earthquake. The care packages were returned to us when the children graduated from preschool. Still, if a writer cannot write a simple note as a parental duty, what meaning is there in the words she does write?

A few days ago, I got an email from my former student who had vowed to dismantle my canon. She said that she was travelling in South America. She mentioned a few things she had learned from our clashes. 'I remember that once you said to us: One must want to be great in order to be good. To this day I still wonder why you looked sad when you said that,' she wrote.

Under what circumstances had I said that? And sad about what? Had she written to enlighten me about what real life was, I would have applauded her consistency. Instead, in her long email, she talked about what I had taught her. I, too, had been young then; how could I have taught anyone anything? All will be well all will be well and every kind of thing shall be well, yet I could not even write a lying note to console my children.

Catching Something

Yiyun Li on All Will Be Well

Yiyun Li's stories and novels have won several awards including the PEN/Hemingway Award, the Guardian First Book Award and a Windham Campbell Prize. She has been contributing stories to The New Yorker since 2003.

In our conversation, we talked about how her writing had changed, about the nature of fiction, and about loss.

What was your starting point and original intention for this story?

Lily's story had been in my head for a long time. Part of it was based on a real hairdresser I used to go to who liked to tell me stories. At the time, I didn't really think about it too much but it *was* strange that I didn't change hairdressers – she wasn't even a good hairdresser, she just wanted to tell me stories. I was always tickled by my wishy washiness.

When we moved away, I no longer went to that hairdresser. But her stories stayed with me and so I always thought that maybe I'd write her story. I even had a title for it: 'Lily Dreams.' But I never wrote it. There was something missing. It was one woman telling another woman stories. It went on for ten years, not writing that story.

And then, a few years later, I was talking to the writer A.M. Homes. I told her that, when my children went to preschool in

California, every year we had to send a care package in case of a catastrophic earthquake. In the care package you were supposed to write a note to say 'Mummy and Daddy will be back,' even though we might be dead by then. I wasn't able to write it. I found it difficult to imagine the children reading this posthumous note.

A.M. Homes said, 'Oh my God, you've got to write this as a story. I need to read it.' Which was when this story occurred to me; sometimes you accumulate these little things from your life and from other people's lives that don't appear immediately to be part of the same story. I knew the story ended with that line, 'all will be well,' and that the narrator would not be able to write the note.

I realised then that Lily's story and the narrator's story were enmeshed. That's why I could not write Lily's story: because I did not have the narrator's story in mind at the time. The story was two women's narratives intersecting at a strange angle, the imbalance of what they tell each other, and what they tell the reader. Lily is a very willing storyteller, while the narrator is reluctant to give away anything. The story is really about that imbalance, how time passes, and the two women's different dreams. Then I started to write the story and it was quite easy to write once I had figured that piece out.

Did you start writing at what is now the beginning?

I did. I always write from the beginning to the end. When I knew what the story was, I started with: 'Once upon a time...' I wish I could start all my stories with 'Once upon a time...' but this is the one story in which you can do that. I started with Lily's story and weaved in the narrator's story.

You've said in an interview that you wanted to write about a public space, like I. B. Singer's 'The Cafeteria.' What is it about the nature of Lily's salon that is important in this story?

'The Cafeteria' is a superb story. Reading that, I thought: *that's how I want to write a story.* Lily's is like all hair salons or cafeterias – it's a place to collect people: all these uncles and aunts, who sit there and watch tv dramas and read newspapers. I always liked those places; in hair salons especially, the hairdresser and the customer are performing. One is always more talkative than the other so there's always an imbalance. Talking equally is not interesting. No one is going to write a story about two people having an equal amount of airtime.

A hair salon is interesting because it can make people so self-conscious. While the uncles and aunts are simply talking, it's like the narrator is auditioning to be someone else. I don't like my characters to be as internal as I am – I like to push them out into the world and a hair salon is a natural place for that.

Even though the narrator doesn't participate particularly well in the performance?

I think there's some uneasiness within the narrator, while Lily has all these stories – there is some sort of assuredness in being able to tell a stranger your life story. I really admire Lily.

The narrator moves between a number of poles: she is attracted to and repulsed by stories; warms to and shies from danger; symbolises the Western canon to her student and an American devil to Lily, though was brought up in China. Did you know these tensions in her before you wrote the story or did you discover them as you wrote?

I did not have these things in mind when I started writing. There was a 'Lily' in my head: she was someone from real life who I fictionalised. But the narrator wasn't in my head. I didn't know the things you mentioned about her.

Usually, I wouldn't feel comfortable writing about someone who is a writer, or a writing teacher with experience close to mine. I shy away from writing autofiction. So in order to write the narrator, part of the struggle was leaving behind this instinct to not write about myself and instead to say, 'I really *need* to write this narrator – even though she is unwilling to talk about herself, she can't only be this voice telling someone else's story.'

I didn't know any of these things about her. I didn't want her to be too self-reflective, but just to present her contradictions simply. The narrator's gaze is outward: she avoids looking at herself – it's there even in her decision to visit this salon and not to drive twenty minutes to a safer neighbourhood. Which, by the way, was also something from my life. I went to a hair salon in a bad neighbourhood but never asked myself why; it was a decision I'd made and I had to stick with it.

But, no, I did not know all these contradictions in the narrator until I started writing.

And were you surprised?

I was surprised that she made up this whole lie about being adopted by someone in the Netherlands. Who *was* she to tell those lies?! It wasn't even good fiction – they were just lies. I was fascinated that she kept on doing that. The narrator has a little bit of overlapping experience with my life; she had a childhood like mine in Beijing but she was so different to me. I was a little bit in awe that she would go on telling these blatant lies.

From which the story explores the nature of fiction and 'lies' and life?

Maybe Lily is telling the whole truth about her life. But sitting in that chair, and having already told these lies about herself, the narrator cannot trust Lily 100% and so the reader might not trust Lily.

When you tell your stories how much do you embellish? How much detail do you give to your stories? I am fascinated by that: the stories we tell and how we lie about ourselves.

Did you know that the narrator was writing this after the loss of a son?

Yes, I did. I was writing this story after my son died and so was very much aware of how it felt to be in that place. I knew the narrator was writing at a time of mourning about a sunnier place, California, and a sunnier time when the children were younger.

Yes, I was aware of that and I knew that the story would turn really hard when she says, 'I lost my son.'

I'm sorry I didn't know. That was insensitive of me.

No, it is fine. It is part of my life.

Are you okay to go on?

Yes, of course, it is fine.

Ok. Near the end of the story, the narrator says, 'all I wanted was to keep the unknown, good or bad, at a distance.' Does this buffer between herself and the harshness of the world suggest she was coping with a tragedy even in that early time, or maybe that the narrator mistakenly attributes her current grief to this earlier period in her life?

Yes and no. It's interesting you pick up on this line – we can't say with 100% assurance that she's talking about her earlier self, because when things change and things happen in life, it puts you in a different position: you start to rewrite yourself, start to revise your script about the earlier time.

So, in a way, she *is* talking from a point of grief, saying that earlier, 'I had this instinct to do these things because I knew what was coming in my life.' They may not be true but you can never discount it – in life, there's always a little bit of truth there. Whether she is or isn't mistaken is a fuzzy point.

What is it like writing something semi-intentionally fuzzy? Do you know you're doing it at the time: strumming a chord instead of playing one note?

Yes, I think so. In general, I write with absolute clarity and hope for absolute clarity for the reader. This happens not to be one of these stories. In this story, I was intentionally not differentiating one shade of truth or lie from another. Because, yes, this is something you can do when writing a story, which is the beauty of writing a story and when it works, it works.

If this was a departure for you, does it mean this wasn't a mode you stuck with?

I feel like this story possibly went against a *lot* of my writer's beliefs; for instance, I usually do not write in first person because I find that challenging – although I have to say I am using first person more and more, maybe as I learn from my own experience. But you have to make certain allowances.

I think the story was meaningful to me in a way that doesn't show for the reader because it's a story where I use my own life as material and put in those moments where I walked with the children when they sung that Australian gum tree song, or when they were going to preschool and I had to write those almost 'suicide note' letters. The whole concept had been so heartbreaking I'd blocked the memory out before.

But as a writer at some point you have to step up and say, 'yes, I'm going to use this material.' Even though it's extremely painful for me, it makes a compelling story. There's no reason to avoid those things.

Do you think the lack of clarity you were working towards was an avoidance of the autofiction? To not put yourself so fully in the picture?

Autofiction is a fuzzy thing for me. For example, going back to Singer's story again, the narrator's life overlaps with Singer's life story, and yet he didn't give away much about himself. He was mostly describing other people in that cafeteria, with brief moments when he reveals himself, when he says things like: 'I need to write these stories to make some more dollars,' and makes fun of himself.

I feel like there are always more interesting things in the world than I can imagine – my life is less interesting to me than other people's and other people's stories.

We cannot say this is a story about the narrator but we cannot also say this is a story about Lily – it's a story about Lily's crystal-clear life story overlaid with some sort of muddled story that the narrator doesn't tell enough to the readers. That's why it has these ambiguities.

And was it this overlaying structure that explored ideas about the nature of story, so that the reader is very quickly into the enormity of the themes?

I don't know if I was conscious of that but I knew I felt I'd got the story right. When I wrote it I thought, *this is good enough.*

Could you tell me what you mean by 'getting it right'? Or is it impossible to describe a feeling like this?

No, no, our job is to answer questions that are unanswerable.

When I was a young writer, I would think: *I've got it right* and oftentimes I don't think I had. When I was thinking about getting it right back then, it was always the craft: 'I got the point of view right, the pacing was perfect, it's a perfect product.' When you are younger, you strive for stories to be perfect that way. But, if you look at a tree, a real tree always has a few imperfect leaves. It's only with a fake tree that every leaf is perfect.

Now, when I think a story is 'right', I think: *this story has a life.* It doesn't matter if I change a word here or change a transition or plot twist. All those craft points fall away a little when the story is right. So maybe more recently, when I think about getting it right, I only think about capturing the story.

So instead of consciously 'thinking' about craft, how would you describe the process?

I almost want to say 'unthinking' but that's not right either. Craft is about thinking and making decisions and I feel what I'm doing now is not about making decisions; it's about catching something. And whatever way you catch that thing is good.

When I was younger I felt it was easier for me to talk about writing because I knew what I was doing. I knew the decisions I made. Now, it's all just *here.*

So the explicit skills have now become implicit in you?

Maybe from experience there's a lot of things you absorb. You're still making decisions and you're still thinking about craft but you're not consciously spending a lot of time going through these decisions. *Should I do this in the first person or third person? What is the back story?* You stop thinking about all those things. They are part of the nature of storytelling now.

Lily says, 'he said he would wait for me all his life' and, 'he has three daughters and I have three sons.' What was important for you in your writing of Lily's story?

I changed a lot of things from the real hairdresser's life story. Lily's story is a Hollywood story. It's so full of extreme drama you can almost hear the background music. It's nearly a cliché but she saves it with all these astonishing details – all of his three daughters are named after her, and her photo is up in his bedroom. I'm sorry for laughing, it's so painful. That I did not change, I did take that from life because it was one of those things you cannot make up. Life is so much stranger. It is the most painful thing for me to think about that photo there. And yet, when I saw the photo, I understood why it was in the bedroom. Lily's story is an education for the narrator because it has an arc. Life does not really have an arc, Lily's story fits more within that melodramatic Hollywood mould. It was an education for me; even the most clichéd melodrama is a good story if you can tell it in a way that stays with the audience.

And yet the narrator is encouraging us to disbelieve it?

Yes, the narrator lies about herself – the truth about her life is that she doesn't say anything about her dead child – and all the contradictory forces within her make her the worst audience for Lily's story.

What's interesting is Lily has decided she will tell the narrator her story not knowing she's the worst possible audience. Life is strange in that sense. We make decisions and stay with them. Sometimes knowing but still not caring they're bad decisions.

Is that at the centre of the story? Lily and the narrator's misunderstanding?

It's a part of the story. They're not each other's friends; they're actually the wrong audience for each other, and yet they get stuck together in this moment for a period of time. The funny thing is Lily has a husband and three sons, an entire busy life which she *doesn't* talk about. What she doesn't talk about is interesting to me, in the same way the narrator doesn't talk about *her* life. It's too bad that they're stuck in this mould, telling each other stories.

Which I wonder if the narrator notices, when she says she thinks Lily is casting a spell on her?

Right, Lily is a good storyteller in that she does not tell the whole story in one sitting. She drags it out and offers the photo towards the very end as evidence of this tremendous love story. I think: *Oh my God, those two children.* They did look like children who are going to be sacrificed, like they're going to burn these two children.

I remember when I read the story, I found that sentence astonishing. Could you say a little more about this image the narrator gives?

Earlier you asked if I surprised myself, well the moment I wrote that was surprising. So much of the story is about two adult women talking but it is really about how children survived or did not survive their tremendous tragedies.

I always think children are monumental but we don't realise it. We imagine them the size they are and hope they can outlive that little person to become a big person. Just look at Lily and the boy at the moment that photograph was taken. When I was writing that, I realised that if you look at that couple at that moment, their story is as astonishing as anything that has been written in literature: they did not know that they were so pure and so tragic in that picture, so of course I was thinking about my own son when I was writing that: when you lose a child you realise a child cannot always be monumental, which was a striking moment for me. I realised then I wasn't only writing about Lily and the narrator but also about the children and all the tragedy in their lives.

I really enjoyed the story's discussion of how life and story interact. How *consciously* were you exploring and illuminating this theme?

Very consciously I think. Although, not as conscious as though I'd said: 'I'm going to do this,' I was more conscious of *where* I was as I was writing that story. When A.M. Homes told me I should write about that episode when my children were younger, I realised later what she meant and felt very conscious of where I was.

You asked before why did you go away from my usual mode: you always have to try something you didn't know you could do, so writing that story was the right thing to do.

This exploring of the nature of story recurs throughout; it's in her argument with the student, it's in her almost-contradictory attitude to Lily; it occurs everywhere and everywhere there's a new depth or angle or light shining on it. Was making the narrator's job a creative writing teacher intentionally adding a new dimension to this exploration?

Yes, I was conscious that the profession of the narrator is important for the story. When I'm teaching writing, I always think I'm going to fail. How can you teach I.B. Singer's story, for example? I teach that all the time and the students fall short in their understanding of it, and I fall short in my teaching it. You can never live up to the story you're teaching.

Your striving and never perfectly grasping the story, it reminds me of a quote from the narrator when she's teaching – 'One must want to be great in order to be good.' Is there a connection here, and is this a statement that you hold to?

Yes and no. I think I must *have* said that to a student early on because that email is an adaptation of an email I got from a student

– she *had* said I looked tired when I said that. Which must mean that I used to believe in that. I would say that. And when she described how tired I looked, I thought, *what do you mean I look tired, of course I look tired, I was the mother of young children, I was not sleeping.*

Yes, I believe in that to a certain extent, though at the moment, even to be good is a high standard. I don't want to be great, I want to be good. Lots of times, if you can say that something is good, for me, that's very high praise.

You finish the story with 'All will be well all will be well and every kind of thing shall be well, yet I could not even write a lying note to console my children.' Why did you make *this* the last sentence?

Because, for one, that quote has always stayed with me for years and years. That is one thing we do as parents, we say, 'everything is going to be all right, everything will be well,' otherwise how do we bring up children into the bleak world?

And coming back to what a writer can and cannot do; a writer cannot write a lying note to her own children because that is beyond her. I wanted to end on a storyteller failing to tell a story, failing their most important assignment: that's meaningful, that's life. When we talk about failure, any time you fail at what you do the best, it's interesting. It's also heart-breaking.

An aside from that story, it always amazes me that other parents *could* write that note. It's beyond my imagination how you can write a note like that to a child – it's possibly the last thing they will hear from you!

Did it also work in the framework of the story that it started with 'Once upon a time' and ended with her silence?

I've realised that, when I started to write that story, it came easily from beginning to end. I did not do any revision because I knew I'd got it by the end of that last sentence.

I think the fact that something came to you so instinctively holds up to such interrogation is magic, for want of a better word.

If we had discussed another story, I would have said 'I did *this* because this was my intention' or 'that was why I did that.' This story just doesn't have those sidenotes. It came as the story – I believe in that, that a good story should simply be alive. I still think that writing is chasing something, catching it in its being, rather than 'assembling' something.

Which is also what I'm interested in with these interviews; that you did something not fully conscious and yet its outcome formed something beyond your immediate understanding.

I think that might be a good way to put it.

What, if anything, did you learn about short story craft in the writing of this story?

I don't want to sound arrogant but after this story, writing has become a little less technical for me. After this one, I knew to trust my instinct.

And before that you were less trusting and therefore edited more?

Before this story, I still trusted my instinct but oftentimes there would be a moment when I'd think: *wait a moment, something is not quite right, maybe I should take this paragraph out to fix the pacing or maybe change the point of view here* – as if thinking technically might solve the problem. Now I know a story is written sentence by sentence not decision by decision.

Bulk

by Eley Williams

We were all on the beach for different reasons when we found the whale. The moon was still up and the morning was cold enough that our conversations could be seen writ faintly in the air above our heads as breaths met in the early winter sky. It appeared first as threads from our lips that briefly formed one shape, connective and fragile like a wishbone.

I remember looking at my watch as I approached and saw it was not yet seven o'clock.

I am not too sure how many of us in total were gathered there staring at the whale's body – fewer than ten, let's say. In many ways I am an imperfect eyewitness. I was close enough to have been able to make out all of their features in the bad light, the good dark, but at the time such a thing seemed unimportant. I slipped a little on a hand of bladderwrack as I scuttled over the rocks to join the knot of bystanders standing on the shoreline.

'Do you think we can push it back?' someone was asking the group as I arrived. Whether out of reverence or an absurd sense that something so big and so dead might be eavesdropping on us, disapproving of our small lives and concerns, we all spoke to each other in eking whispered slivers.

'It's long gone,' came an answer. The man speaking wore stout, expensive, too-clean boots and his vowels sounded well-rested and alert. 'I tried to get closer earlier, and the gulls or the crows have already taken its eyes. I only left for a moment to fetch my camera from home,' he went on, 'but I spotted you all moving in so I thought that I should come back.'

'They drown in air,' said a young woman who was closest to me. She was carrying a metal flask and leaning against the man on her other side. One could tell immediately that this couple had not yet been to bed and were not entirely sober – they used their hands too much when they spoke and stood swaying in evening clothes that were not doing them favours in the frosty sea-breeze. They smiled at each other constantly and shared looks over their shared flask while the rest of us stared ahead at the whale in the water.

'Drown in air?' echoed her young rumpled man, unconvinced and affectionate.

'It happens,' she insisted. She gnawed on the wool of his jacket.

'*One* of us did well in their biology exam,' he said, and he looked at the rest of us for congratulation. 'Got seventy six percent! Marks back just last week.'

The young woman, feigning embarrassment, added, 'Out of a hundred,' and then looked around at us too, and pulled the man closer to her side.

As we murmured responses without knowing why, I noticed that another one of our group seemed to be crying. She had a flask in her hands too. No, look again – it was not a flask, it was an urn. Perhaps she thought that this time in the morning would be a good quiet moment to come down to the beach and find it empty enough for her purposes. I patted my pocket for tissues but I had not set out on my drive this morning prepared for whales nor mourners.

'Have you had a drink up there, at the hotel?' the young man was asking me. Some gulls overhead began wheedling and wheeling, making jagged chevrons of the sky with their shoulders. 'The guy behind the bar tried to serve me a Martini with a glacé cherry in it.'

'I live next door to there,' I said in case he had seen me the previous evening and was trying to place my face. He assessed me blearily but closely. He leaned further in, speaking over his companion's hair. 'This one here – I love her so much. I love her loads,' he said, and he squeezed his arm about her waist but kept his eyes on me. I said nothing and he interpreted this as a prompt. His voice was still a whisper and it sang with alcohol. 'She worms into you the way that smoke gets into your hair.' He nodded and would not stop nodding until I nodded too. His eyes dropped to the plastic bag in my hands.

When I first saw the whale from the road, I had pulled over into a layby and broken into a run without closing the car door as if I thought that I could be of any possible physical use or as if being the first to the scene might afford me special privileges later down the line. As I made my way along the shoreline I tripped over the remnants of a picnic that had been left among the dunes. There was a newspaper, some bunched tinfoil, a blue plastic bag and an abandoned packet of digestives. I had stopped and tidied the mess together, and noticed that the newspaper's crossword was completed with a thick red marker pen; the clues had been ignored and instead every box was filled with the name ANNA ANNA ANNA ANNA both *Across* and *Down*. A neat coven of ants had arranged itself around the rim of a discarded biscuit too, headbutting it and worrying at its crumbs. They were working around the biscuit's circumference in a slow-moving country dance so I let them have it and made my way over to the people looking at the soft-bucking surf and its whale.

'Is this yours?' I said, shaking the bag, and the man recoiled.

The morning light had a silky, pearly menace to it and I could feel the salt on my lips. Another member came skittering across the rocks to swell our group. He had a small dog at his feet, a wiry, teddybearish breed that looked frayed at the edges. The dog kept to our line and regarded the whale with a very frank expression while the owner comforted the woman who was carrying the urn.

'We didn't know where you had gone,' he said to her. He looked as if he too had been crying all night.

By now the other man with the stout boots had clocked the urn-holding and as the dog-owner held the woman, stout-boots said something in a low voice that was calculated to be calming. I did not quite hear the beginning of his sentence because the wind changed and a gull gave a loud cry, but watching all three faces involved I knew that he should probably shut up. In the next moment the wind changed again and I heard him conclude, ' – and when we scattered him it changed the pH levels in the soil so the next year the hydrangeas were blue instead of pink.' They allowed him to finish, and then the woman with the urn and the man with the dog glared at the stout-booted man so he looked over to meet my eye, then eyed the bag of rubbish in my hand disapprovingly.

'I want to touch it,' the girl in the evening-wear said, and she broke from our line to move towards the body of the whale. The young man pulled her back by the sleeve of her dress, gently – she shook him off, annoyed, but did not advance any further.

'Do you think it's warm?' I heard her say. 'I can't believe it doesn't smell.'

I was acutely aware of my work lanyard around my neck and, as she spoke, I stowed it away under my jumper.

'I bet it would make this sound if you rubbed it,' said her companion. He made a high-pitched squeaky-honking noise, *whgeehh wheeghh wghheehh.*

'I bet it feels like an aubergine under water when you wash it. When you wash them,' said the woman with the urn. The younger woman took another pull of her flask and the man with the dog dipped his chin beneath his scarf more snugly.

'Like an aubergine,' the drunk man repeated, and we all heard the giggle rising through his line.

'Or like a wellington boot,' said the woman with the urn.

After a while, in an attempt to break the mood the man with the stout-boots and well-rested voice said, 'Last year, someone was throwing a ball for their dog over on those cliffs up there. They were telling me all about it at the hotel bar. Someone was throwing the ball and the dog bringing it back. Throwing the ball, the dog bringing it back. They threw the ball once more and the dog went for it again but they had miscalculated... the ball went over the cliff edge and the dog just went with it, right over.'

We all turned and looked at the red and white cliffs looming over the beach. They looked like wine-stained teeth and all our footsteps led from them. I could hear my car's alarm alerting me to its open door.

The younger woman stretched out her hand in the whale's direction and traced the outline of the whale in the air. Her friend kept a grip on her elbow but, sensing that she was distracted he leaned in closer to me again. His breath was full and wobbly as he inclined his head towards his companion. 'When she paid for the drinks last night,' he said, conspiratorially, 'she used the–' and the man extended his hand out, crooking his fist and demonstrating, '*this* part to punch the number in the machine rather than the tips of her fingers. The knuckles. Punch punch punch.'

'Maybe she's worried about germs,' I said.

'Indicative,' he said unsteadily, and then he reeled his friend in and kissed the top of her head. We all looked back to the whale lying in the surf.

After a few minutes of collective silence, the man with the stout, too-clean boots piped up. 'I have seen dead whales explode on TV,' he said. 'They swell up with the gas caused by the bacteria and then, *boom*!, guts everywhere just showering down. It happens quite often.' This man's voice was very well-to-do and the way that he said the word *often* meant that it would rhyme with *orphan*. Perhaps this was the reason that the drunk couple began openly giggling. It was a beautiful voice – as if the stout-booted man was giving an a cappella of speech, rather than just talking – but it seemed so performed and out of place. The gulls wheeled closer above our heads.

'Are you from around these parts?' the woman with the urn asked the stout-booted man. She seemed to have dried her eyes and was looking a lot better. The dog, sitting now at my feet, kept its nose pointing at the body of the whale with the same rapt expression.

'I'm one of the people living this month up at the bothy,' said the stout-booted man, and he pointed up at the cliffs again. 'Perhaps you've seen the posters.'

'The *converted* bothy,' the woman with the urn corrected him, and the stout-booted man coughed. The drunk couple laughed again into their sleeves. I knew a little about the cottage he meant. Draughty with cold walls and the kind of cheap paper lampshades that look like pale globes or imitation moons or a thin-skinned grub suspended from a wire. I had visited one of the artists there, invited to stay the night after some cleric-collared pints together at the clifftop glacé cherry hotel. It was nice enough inside and nice enough company. As I got dressed in the morning, I remember that I had looked out at their view of the sea and at their cocoon-lampshade, and I could not help but think about my beetles waiting for me at work. As I looked again at the whale and followed this thought, I recalled the smooth metal dish that had sat on the bothy's windowsill. The artist in residence at the time had called from their residency by the bed that this dish was a Tibetan singing bowl. They confessed that they had been using the Tibetan singing bowl as an ashtray, and I had thought about my beetles at work again and the clacking of their scales and frass.

'Did you say whales *explode*?' the woman with the urn asked the group. Out of politeness to the stout-booted artist and his facts about whales we all took a step back from the water's edge and its cargo. As they retreated, the sleepless, rumpled couple let their giggles grow louder and the air swelled with the largeness of a laugh and changed the format of the whale-near breeze.

The man with the dog had turned to me and was asking me directly. 'Yes. Is that true about the explosions? You'd know all about it, I expect, you being–' and he mimed something that denoted professionalism while also taking in the bulk of the whale with a sweep of his arm. The group's heads all turned across to look at me, to search me up and down. The dog shifted against my shin, embarrassed on my behalf at the attention, and his owner pointed at my neck, presumably at the just-visible purple cord of my lanyard. 'I saw your ID card. You're from the museum, aren't you? Fossils and that.'

I don't know a thing, I wanted to say. *I am not very clever but I am affectionate about knowledge. Let's start there.* I had started driving around the coastal roads at four that morning because I could not sleep for fear of dreaming about the beetles, and I had hoped that the thrum of the engine and the blank, banked hedges of the roadsides would helped calm me down or make the idea of my coming day and its silent beetles bearable.

'Natural history museum,' explained the man with the dog to the woman with the urn, and everyone nodded and looked at me again expectantly.

'What should we do?' asked the man with the dog.

'Police?' asked the woman with the urn.

'Ambulance?' asked the girl with the flask. She and her friend and the gulls collapsed again with laughter.

I wanted to tell them that I did have a professional stake in the whale and that I should be the one to call it in. I wanted to tell them that I oversaw the dim rooms on the museum's second floor, rooms that were not open to any visitors and certainly not if visitors were to try to enter carrying urns and flasks and frank-faced little dogs. We keep three beetle colonies there in big glass tanks, I wanted to tell them. The colonies pick apart any organic material that is placed in with them. They surge forward and over and under and through, and strip every scrap away, right down to the bone. It is clean work. It is so much better to use dermestid beetles in this way to whisk flesh and matter from specimens so that they can be prepared for exhibition – it is certainly the quickest and the cheapest method, and boiling can destroy the cartilage.

I wanted to tell them what a gift the sea had given them and I moistened my lips, twisting somebody else's plastic bag in my hands, but the wind changed a third time and I could not bring myself to speak against it. The ill-dressed young man beside me gave a shiver and used his shirtsleeve to wipe his mouth.

When I watch them at work, the movement of my beetles across the specimens seems so fluid and neat. I can't imagine a beetle being cowed by a whale's size and I wondered if the museum would be able to find a tank big enough if the cuts are made the right way. I wondered whether beetles ever suffer from insomnia, or think beetle-thoughts about huge bodies of water with something like gratefulness.

'I *will* touch it!' declared the young woman suddenly with a renewed vigour and she slipped from her partner's arm and ran in an arc out towards the head of the whale, picking out a route over the rocks with shoeless feet. There was an ungainliness about her small size next to the great bulk of the whale. There was an imbalance to the scene on the shoreline generally, as if a note was being sung off-key or somewhere a pair of parentheses had been left unclosed.

I had the number that I should call for moments just like this stored in my phone. There are procedures I knew I should be following – I knew that I should look at the whale and see logistics and admin. I thought about the mitral valves that would be exposed, named after the bishop's hat they resemble, and I thought about the sight of actual heartstrings that are as long as your arm, and imagined them being pulled cherry-bright against the bruising water and cloud-damp. I thought about striped chalky cliffs and the texture of the metal bowl hidden up there on a windowsill, sitting with its curled cooling cigarettes lying dusty at its centre. If I made the phone call, I knew that men and women would arrive in the appropriate branded vans with matching plastic outfits and small logos on the chest. Men and women with saws and chainmail gauntlets on their arms to protect their flesh as they set to work. I thought about the baleen of the whale's mouth, thick as horsehair, and the meat that would be shown to the sky. The fact that this meat would be dark with oxygen, almost black – darker than venison or duck – while the blubber would be a white tinged a pale pink. I know your underbellies, I think, as I looked at the whale and at the watchers of the whale – I know the spread of your systems when they are all laid out and spread on a table or against the rocks. There is a heart there big enough for me to lie upon and sleep and not touch the rocks if I curled up with my knees tucked under my jaw. If the men and women arrive it will take three tractors just to drag the body up the beach and flip it over. I know the procedures involved, I think, and that they might loop a thick chain around the whale's heart once they get to it. The tractors would then have to heave it along the rocks, scrabbling for purchase with their tough treads on, along the rocky shore.

I fixed my eyes on the whale in the water and continued to pass the blue plastic bag between my hands. The gulls made their thoughts clear on the matter and waited for my answer. Above us and above the gulls, the morning's just-visible moon pulled the sea an inch inwards as if for a waltz.

There is a Pursuit

Eley Williams on Bulk

'Bulk' is taken from Eley Williams' collection Attrib. *(Influx Press, 2017), which was awarded the Republic of Consciousness Prize and the James Tait Black Memorial Prize 2018.*

This interview was originally conducted by email, although Eley also agreed to a further video conversation some months later. In our discussions, she talked about how her writing style is influenced by her previous story, and not being 'hot on plot.'

How did this story originally come to you? Was the image of the beached whale the starting point?

My sister is a zoologist, currently living in Denmark. In the course of a phone conversation peppered with small talk, she casually mentioned that one of her duties that week was to pop up and assist with the removal of a dead beached whale and perform a cetacean biopsy on it. She described the strangeness of the scene, its skewed sense of perspectives, the disruption to the normal patterns of the day, the use of a local fishing museum to supply requisite saws and gauntlets.

The story really is drawn from a central sensation – rather than an image – that she described. Down the phone, she told me that as she reached into the opened body of the whale to haul at its tendineae (colloquially known as the 'heart strings'), she could hear the wind whistling through the cords and there was an audible note, as if the whale had been turned into a huge Aeolian harp in her hands. I wanted to nod to this sense of the mythic and the absurd as well as the incidental or familiar in this story.

Some openings seek to unsettle or defamiliarise – this one uses some very explicitly *establishing* sentences, as if to set out the parameters of an investigation. It reminded me of one writer's approximating of a short story to an essay, its conclusion the unwritten effect in the reader.

I wondered if this idea had any parallel in your work?

Yes, certainly in this story. When so much of the power of a story is its treatment of ambiguity – the trailings off and suggestions of tonal meaning that may differ from reader to reader – I suppose 'explicit' is a good word because I did not want the brute fact of the whale to be ambiguous. This story is about confrontation and I wanted the different people looking at one definite strange thing to be the clearest set parameter for confrontation.

I like the styling of it as an essay but I suppose with the proviso that a good essay will be discursive and provide a lot of evidence to suggest a logical conclusion; I wouldn't want a short story necessarily to have one strict meaning or to forward an argument to convince a reader necessarily. But yes, the idea of a starting premise or a clear scene setting was important to this story and I hope the figure of the whale provided that.

On the fourth page of the story, you move from the *in media res* opening to give a description of the background context to the scene: 'When I first saw the whale from the road, I had pulled over...'

How did you decide *when* to sequence this 'explainer' here?

I think it's to do with the previous question – a crucial theme for the story was confrontation, so I started with that moment. If this was to be a scene in a novel, I would have wanted to start by foregrounding how it would be momentous. I think the short story feels like a good fit for a combination of immediacy and confrontation. I like the idea of a reader needing to work out what is surface and what is an instinctive reaction from the narrator without knowing much about the characters.

Often in my stories, my characters are uncertain and the reader has to work out in the moment what they will do next. In this instance, if I was to give more of a backstory and not front-load it with realisation like this, some of this momentum would be lost here.

On the subject of the narrator's uncertainty, you have described your narrator as 'over-thinking, or getting snagged in networks of over-association and dis-association.' What effect did you want to have with this writing style?

Uncertainty is not necessarily about 'unreliability', or teasing the reader in terms of how far they can trust (or distrust, or mistrust) the narrator's account. A huge whale on a beach *should* be 'the elephant in the room' or the 'dead cat on the table' for the characters who are suddenly only able to see themselves in terms of their proximity to it or the status they can assume in terms of controlling what happens next.

I thought it might be more interesting, therefore, for the circumstances in 'Bulk' to be experienced and expressed in terms of the askance or the tentative, rather than the direct, clear or pragmatic.

You describe one character's actions in the story with: 'He nodded and would not stop nodding until I nodded too.'

When you create your characters, do you empathise *from* their inner emotions *out*, to chart their actions? Or, here, I wondered if you were simply 'seeing' the character and working exclusively on the outside?

This short story presents strangers put together, people who are unfamiliar with others' actions; they might be physical tics or strange rituals; they don't know whether they're spontaneous or strange blurts or freakish utterances, so they're having to do a lot of watching.

Even when you are engaged in surveillance, you can still make a connection, so there's a strange intimacy in watching someone very closely without being sure yet of the other person's either literal or physical vocabulary. Which is why many of the characters have to really concentrate on the surface.

You have said a goal of yours can be to make the dialogue convincingly unconvincing. Why do you aim for this effect?

People express themselves in deliberate, mannered, precise ways as often as they communicate in non-verbal ways, or confusing ways, or illogical ways. Some people say more with a breath than they would in a soliloquy.

How to ensure the mood, as well as the phrasing, is coherent? Writing dialogue sometimes has to be a mix of approximating a fictional transcript and not being overly elusive, allusive or abrupt so that it doesn't overwhelm the reader with unnecessary guesswork. Written text permits a certain amount of suspension of disbelief on the part of the reader at the best of times, or tolerance of a base-level editorial intrusion (the accepted upholstery of inverted commas, 'correct' grammar, syntax, punctuation, spelling, etc). Perhaps the best I could aim for was making speech patterns recognisable.

I wondered if the characters were more performative because of the audience of the whale?

Yes, these are people who would not usually talk to one another – if they were to acknowledge one another it would be in a nodding acquaintance, which is a different sort of required choreography. But they're *having* to react, and those who want to establish a hierarchy of power will come to the fore, meaning others will move to the background.

Having a whale as provocation means they have to say something. Having something stark and irrefutable for this story felt important. It meant that characterisation was forced upon the characters; they had to claim space for themselves amongst people who, if it was an otherwise empty beach, they could avoid.

Is this something you came to as you were writing, or a device you planned in order to bring about this communion and make their characteristics explicit?

I knew when I was writing it that I wanted the whale to be a central conceit. A lot of my stories are about individuals having a crisis, either of confidence or faith or communication or passion. I don't often have them actively interacting with other people, so I knew I wanted this story to be more populous instead of just someone in suspended – begrudging or otherwise – animation.

My drafting would have started with me considering: *how will the narrator confront the idea of the whale?* Which will then have developed into: *what will then happen if other people are introduced? How might this be a way to learn more about the narrator and how they might feel beholden to or potentially in control of other people's access to a moment that might have otherwise been a private encounter?*

In my collection *Attrib.*, the stories' narrators aren't usually in positions of power, they are more curational or background figures, so the fact that the narrator has to consider the strangers in terms of the foreground came during the writing of it, rather than being planned out in draft form.

You have said that 'when you write stream-of-consciousness pieces, the problem is how to make the thought complete — without it being a ricochet of constant energies.' Did you face this dilemma writing 'Bulk'? How did you work to overcome it?

I think parts of 'Bulk' concentrate upon the requirement for tasks or roles: who is going to do something about this whale? Who is able to? Who is going to have to ask for help? Even if this state of affairs causes tension or friction, there is a pursuit or a direction rather than being meandering or illustrative.

Which reminds me of Edgar Allan Poe's prescription that a story is above all a unity. With this 'pursuit', do you think the disparate voices in this story come together to form a unified, coagulated whole?

That word 'coagulation' I really like. It has a sort of amorphousness to it as a word, a sort of clagginess that feels perhaps how I draft a story; it doesn't feel like a clean construction, it feels like stuff is intruding onto an idea.

It reminds me of an article about an oil painting of a coastline ['Restoration Reveals Hidden Whale in 17th Century Dutch Painting', *The Guardian*, 4 June 2014]. A restorer daubed away at the paint and revealed that the original composition featured a beached whale surrounded by figures. So the purpose of the picture – its unit of narrative – would have been a beached whale and people reacting to it, but by mistake or intention this changed and the new narrative didn't require those figures, didn't require even the whale; it was just the setting and coast that was important. Which has parallels to this story. For example, what I remember most vividly about writing this story was wanting to include the details of the narrator working with beetles. I almost remember the beetles as much as I remember the whale. And thinking about the unit of the short story in the same way, although the beetles could almost have been left out, they inform how I think of the story most importantly.

Similarly, the other characters in the story are interchangeable to an extent. I wanted them to be various and different types of people. It wasn't important to me who they were. I didn't have a picture of them, I just wanted them to be hotching – they had to imbue movement and power dynamics. So, yes, I wanted it to form a unified story but I wanted that to have coagulation and implied energies within the unit because that is what makes it meaningful.

And how did you arrive at these seemingly disparate notions and speeches?

These parts were the ones that I adjusted the most in the drafting process, coming from snatches of dialogue that I had in abstract in my notebook. I wanted this back and forth to make it more interesting, with its varied pace, emotional register and setting up and deflating egos. I think certainly the genders and ages of the people speaking I switched around a lot to see what effects would be different there.

You've said before you're 'not hot on plot.' However, your mentioning of pace and emotion and dramatic shifts all sound like elements of a satisfying short story. Do you think that maybe you are better at plot than you admit?

I'd love to take that Girl Guide badge and stick it on and say: 'I did it, I achieved plot.' I'm just in awe of people who make plots seem easy and I seek out interviews with these authors to find out how they had the brain to write the crossword and solve it and make the reader feel satisfied at this point.

With this story and another one called 'Spines', I thought that what was satisfying about a well-plotted short story was the use of devices to have a certain effect, without relying on emotional intensity through language. I feel comfortable using those devices but is that the same as having an engaging structure with its unveiling and unravelling? It seemed more like an exercise in considering how many of these tick boxes I could apply. It might have some of that 'satisfaction through shape' rather than characters' desire.

But, yes, I was trying desperately.

You've mentioned drafting, how does that work for you?

With this story I would have written down: 'People finding a dead whale on a beach.' Then from there, I'd probably have written a good 8,000 words of unsequenced notes that would occur to me around that central premise. Whether that is just snatches of dialogue or: 'include a cagoule,' or describe the sound as being like 'aubergine under water.'

That will probably happen over a couple of days, just adding to those notes and stray lines. Usually, if I can find a day to sit down with that document, I can sift and arrange and paddle around in it until a structure seems to form.

I wanted there to be a change of pace in this story, not just a scene described and then a tide receding; I wanted the reader to find out if there was something to be worked out in it. While making those notes, I wouldn't know what would be kept and what would be left behind.

You have said that a large amount of your editing is cutting back. What sort of things did you find yourself cutting out for this story?

With this story I did not want the reader to be overly invested in any of the characters and their backstories – it might be useful to know the *why*, *who* and *where* for their appearance, but to delineate or develop their circumstances or motivations would make the story over-elaborate and perhaps a little distracting. I'm all for distraction, but this story was meant to be about encounters rather than corollaries.

Some writers say that they follow the impetus of the language – feeling their way through a story. Others strip back language to give pace and weight to the storyline. Would you put yourself somewhere on this continuum?

I wouldn't say I have a formula or a strategy as I sit down for each individual story. I think it's often dictated by what I did in the last story – if I feel like in one story I'm making the sentences reveal more and more about a character, I will make sure that's not the tactic I'm adopting for the next one.

Can I ask why? Are you challenging yourself? Or is this a sign that you are 'at play' when you write stories?

It'd be great if it did feel like I was playing. It is more an attention or boredom thing. For example, if in one story I set out to attempt to write 'dazzling' sentences, hopefully I will have got that ambition of out my system during the writing process for that story. If I wanted to do the same thing again, I'd think: *why not just make this a continuation of the same story?*

Part of the enjoyment I have in reading a collection of short stories is that you don't have to be in the same narrator's head, you can try new things for new situations.

My hope is I could sit in the middle of those two ends of the spectrum but I suspect in editing I'm more aware of strimming out the language to serve the story, rather than growing a story and working out when I should stop growing.

The story ends with the sentence: 'Above us and above the gulls, the morning's just visible moon pulled the sea an inch inwards as if for a waltz.' Why make this the last sentence?

I think because it's not in keeping with the tone of the rest of the story. A moonlit morning by a coast has a romanticism to it, so the sentence is fittingly lush and rich and poetic where a lot of the story is not: it is about death and creepy crawlies and people being weirded out and almost fighting each other.

But here the conflict is set against the idea of a waltz in which you draw someone in to face you, which is a moment of frisson rather than tension. It allowed me to suggest that a morning by a beach will always be lovely, even if it is full of brusque, blunt, overwhelming scenarios. I suppose I wanted that clash whilst ending with something light.

Hearing it back I'm glad it ended like that. It's neither a twist nor simply about the power struggle. I feel that, rather than seeking out conflict, the reader can put the book down and bring the atmosphere of an ongoing dance into whatever they read next.

To All Their Dues

by Wendy Erskine

Mo

Three types of beauty salon: the pristine Swiss clinic set-up where the staff might as well be in scrubs; tart's boudoir with a job lot of gold leaf and damask; and then the retro parlour with a few framed fifties pin-ups. Mo had tried something different. Tropical. An InvestNI start-up loan and a bit of money she'd saved bought her a tiny shop unit and some second-hand equipment from a liquidation auction. On the two-week start-up course they'd said about how you'd to achieve a total concept with it all working together to create brand synergy – the waiting area, the music, the décor. She had got a mate to do the painting. She had in mind a Caribbean paradise but when he'd finished it looked like a coffee shop off the Damrak. Would you like a quarter with your eyelash tint? Today's double-sell! The lights on dim and it didn't look so bad. The total concept got abandoned. The bowls of sand and shells in the waiting area should have been a good idea but people were always sticking their hands in and making the magazines gritty. After three days of *Classic Reggae: The Soundtrack to Jamaica* on repeat Mo retreated to the usual gentle ambient sounds and filled the bowls with boiled sweets.

What they said on the course didn't matter anyway because it was all about the quality of the treatments. Treatments were reasonably priced – allowing for a careful margin – and methodically executed.

Nails, waxing, facials, bit of massage, fake tan. One treatment room. Total reliability: no day-release wee dolls messing things up. She was in the place for 8, ready to start at 9 and she was there for the rest of the day, six days a week. Mo was starting to get regular clients, which was good. When she opened she'd put an advert in the local free paper with a discount voucher (15%: enough to create a positive vibe) and that had got things started well. She wasn't fully booked at this stage – there were gaps in the diary – but she had known that this was how it would be for at least the first six months.

This morning Mo arrived at the same time as usual. The butcher next door was putting out his sign, a wooden cut-out cow, as Mo put up her metal shutter. Then she went through her routine: kettle on first, switch on the wax pot, light a few of the scented candles (black coconut). You needed to take away the smell of the bleach that lingered from the night before when the whole place had been washed down because ammonia wasn't very ambient. Switch on the heat: important this, although it was expensive. The place always needed to be warm because people felt awkward enough stripping down to paper pants for a tan and they didn't need to be freezing as well. The electric heater made a racket but no one had ever complained. Listen to the answer machine, turn the sign to open and finally, finally make the cup of tea.

Mo was reaching for the milk when there was a shatter of glass. She came through from the back and saw a hole in the window, a circle about two inches wide, and coming from it silver spokes that were tinkling as they crept further towards the edges of the window. Beside the table with the celeb magazines, a shiny red snooker ball had just come to rest. Mo heard the cracking of the glass, stared down at the ball, then looked at the window. Through the hole the road looked darker. She put the ball on the counter and went next door to the butcher's.

Did you hear that? Mo said. My window's just been put in.

The butcher shook his head, continued moving some meat from one tray to another. Shit, he said. That's not good. Do you need a number? For a glass place?

Yes, I do, said Mo. I can't believe that just happened.

Desperate like, he said.

I can't believe that just happened!

A woman came into the shop and he turned his attention away from Mo, did the what can I get for you my darlin?

Waiting at the bus stop outside the salon were a handful of people.

Did you see what happened there? Mo asked them. My window's just been put in.

An old fella shrugged. A boy in school uniform didn't take out his headphones.

Yeah, a man said. Car pulled up and the window went down and they threw something. Drove off quick. Did anybody get hit?

Nobody got hit, said Mo. It was just the window that got wrecked.

Bad state of affairs, said the man. Nuts.

Mo's first client of the day, in for an eyebrow wax and an eyelash tint, never commented on the window.

Blue black? Mo asked.

Blue black, the woman said.

She had taken her shoes off to lie on the bed and they sat neat in the corner, sad little comfortable shoes. Mo mixed the dye in the glass vial then smeared the Vaseline over her eyelids and under her eyes, positioned the semi-circles of paper under her bottom lashes. That window. Unfair so it was. The woman's eyelids fluttered as the dye went on, cold and wet.

That's us, said Mo. I'm going to leave you for ten minutes to let that take. You warm enough? Mo pressed two cotton wool pads on her eyes.

Oh yes, said the woman, lovely.

Good then, said Mo, and she closed the door on the woman lying blind in the dark.

The man from the glass place said he couldn't come out until tomorrow but Mo supposed that was probably as good as she was going to get; she knew that even with the insurance this was going to work out expensive, one way or another. It wasn't a total surprise it happened, she had been expecting something or other. And shouldn't she be thankful that it wasn't something worse, good that it had happened when there weren't any clients around. That fella would call in soon again, she knew it.

Mo went back into the room.

All okay?

Yes, just nodded off, said the woman. Can I stay here the rest of the day?

Mo laughed as she cleaned off the dye, firmly and precisely, and then she handed the woman a mirror to look at the transformation. Before: eyes like a rabbit's, pink and fair. After: it's all the blue black. The woman made her mirror face, an ingénue smile even though she hadn't seen sixty in years.

Oh now that's great. That's great.

The eyebrow wax took seconds, a few swift strokes. Mo mentally calculated her pay per second.

As the woman went out, the butcher came in. Here you might be needing this, he said. We had a bit left over. And he held out a length of glass repair film.

He put it on with only a couple of bubbles rising.

Kids, huh? the butcher said.

Kids, said Mo. That's good of you, I appreciate it. That's great.

Just pay it, he said. Ain't really that much, just pay it.

She hadn't spoken to him before beyond hello. She didn't talk much during the day. Alright, if it was nails, you're facing the person and it's ignorant not to, so you have to talk, but people want to keep it light, holidays and work-dos and new shops that have opened in the town. Other treatments, people just need you to shut the fuck up so let them head off to wherever they want as the cotton wool sweeps over them or your hands smooth their skin with cream. Oh there were questions you could ask if you wanted to, bodies that begged for someone to ask why, what's all that about. That long thin scar, running along the inside of your thigh, lady in the grey cashmere, what caused that? Those arms like a box of After Eights, slit slit slit, why you doing that, you with your lovely crooked smile, why you doing that? The woman with the bruises round her neck, her hand fluttering to conceal them. Jeez missus, is your fella strangling you? But you don't ask, why would you?

Mo had done enough talking, done enough listening. The call-centre job she had done at night while getting the beauty qualification had a boss called Eamonn, a man from Donegal in a velvet jacket. The pay was very poor, he had told her, below the minimum wage, but for every thirty seconds over ten minutes you kept people on the phone you got a bonus. Plus you could work all the hours you wanted pretty much, right into the night. Theresa over there, he pointed at a woman drinking tea from a flask, Theresa earns more than I do. There was a choice: either the sex line or the fortune line. Irish angle on both: guys getting off talking to colleens or women having their future decided by Celtic mystics. The other new girl said, what's with the Irish stuff? I'm not telling some fella I'm Irish when I'm not. You'll just be on the phone, the man from Donegal had said. It'll just be the accent. Which for most people, regardless of your own local distinctions, is Irish. But I'm British, she said. I'm from the loyalist community. Eamonn had looked thoughtful. No, he said. No. That's just too niche. Loyalist psychic readings. Loyalist girls wanting to talk to you now. No, my sweetheart, you are Irish to your fingertips and if you don't like it then that, and he pointed, is the door. She had stayed though and so had Mo. And what would you say, asked Mo, if you were speaking to the fellas? 'Work away there', 'keep working away there' and 'that you finished?' I'm sure you can manage something better, Mo, he had said, if you want to earn any money. Mo was put on the fortune telling. No knowledge of anything spiritual required, said Eamonn. Just keep it sensible and lengthy. If anyone is in severe straits give them the number of the Samaritans. But only after a while.

You could feel them sometimes, people's hopes, even though all you wanted to do was just get on with your job. People looking at their faces, seeing a crumpled version staring back at them, hoping that the dermabrasion was going to make them feel like the time when they were thirty and they told that funny story at their sister's party in that restaurant and everybody laughed. For all this stuff you had to work neatly and quickly: people got nervous if you were hesitant or unsure.

Mo rolled the snooker ball in her hand. Not good. She imagined sitting down in the police station, those concerned faces when she explained what was happening, the offer to make her a cup of tea, the feigned surprise, the commitment that they would do something about it, then nothing, maybe the worse than nothing. Just pay it, the butcher had said. Ain't really that much. Well it really wasn't that much: you could recoup it with a late-night opening. But but but... that would be just the start of it. You could just see the sorry little tale taking shape: next thing it's a friend of mine's daughter needs a job, lovely girl, very keen, all those qualifications in beauty and you don't need anybody but you have to take her, and then the next thing is she arrives, hard piece, lazy-assed piece, and you are stuck with her loafing about and all her friends coming in for mates' rates. The guys next door were paying the money though and Christ knows who else on the road.

Maybe it wasn't any different to insurance. That's what the fella was implying. When he had come in before he had introduced himself and he had shaken her hand. Kyle, he said his name was. There was something about him that let her know that he was not some bloke coming in for a voucher for his missus, the only reason men came to Mo's place. She wasn't doing male treatments, no thank you, she was not doing back, sack and crack, not when she was working by herself, no way. The way he stood there, cock of the walk, like he owned the place.

With this situation there was no a, b and c. It was difficult to know what to do. That was what was wrong with the phone line, idiots wanting advice from spirits or the runes or the stars and yet it was obvious what option they should take. Kick him out! Get out of the flat! Go to a gym! Go to the doctor! Tell her the truth! Give in your notice and look for another job! Can you not understand?

One woman had phoned up about her new dream fella who just didn't get on with her ten-year-old son, had hit him quite hard one time, although fair's fair, the son had been bad, beyond cheeky. Her fella had said that the son was gonna be a problem big-time before too long and she was just so worried about the situation and wondered if she should put the son into temporary foster care, you know just temporary. Couldn't go back to being on her own again.

Pretty obvious what you should do love, isn't it?

What? the woman had said.

I said if you aren't thick as shit it is pretty obvious what you need to do, huh?

Silence on the end of the line.

People like you don't deserve to have kids. You hear that? The stars are saying that, and all the spirits in the spirit world, I can hear them coming through very clearly and they're saying you're a fuckin tool.

Mo didn't need the job any more anyway. She'd got the beauty qualification and the money saved and she was all set: a, b and c.

The next client was a full-body spray tan. Mo showed her into the cubicle where she had laid out the paper pants. White – if it was Marilyn-white, dense and creamy – was beautiful. But people weren't ever Marilyn-white, they were lumpy and mottled. Tan helped but everyone wanted it too brown; never mind the different calibrations Mo offered, they always went for the top intensity. Mo liked doing the spray tan. You needed skill. It wasn't just point and go.

What happened your window? the woman asked, shivering a little as the tan spray moved across her tits.

Mo shrugged, concentrating on progressing to the woman's shoulder blades. Not entirely sure, she said. Young ones messing. It'll be sorted tomorrow. Hopefully anyway.

Terrible, the woman said. A place was burgled the other week.

The man, Kyle, held the door open for the woman on the way out. It gave Mo a shock to see him standing there. He wore a leather suit jacket and held a briefcase that could have come from a game show, the prize bundles inside. He put the briefcase on the table and rested on the counter.

Problem? he asked, nodding towards the window.

It'll be fixed by tomorrow, said Mo, and she started fussing at one of the shelves, aligning moisturisers.

Kyle sighed slowly, shook his head. Not good, he said. This road isn't what it used to be.

Yeah, said Mo.

The other week, he said, I was only trying to help. Seriously. This situation is just what you are trying to avoid. Through the broken glass and the cellophane Mo could just about see a man outside, leaning against a car. She said nothing but put her hands by her sides because shit they were shaking.

You live round here? he asked.

No, said Mo. Well, not that near, she said.

Yeah, you do, said Kyle. House with the white door, number 32. Is there any point in being stupid? he said.

Mo thought of her white door.

He spread himself out in one of the seats. You see, it's like this, he began. It's all about community. Communities don't run themselves. Businesses like yours, they're vulnerable, you see what I mean? There's a lot of people out there who are not nice people and all we are really doing here, you know, if I'm being honest, is offering you our help. As a member of the community.

I know what community means, said Mo.

You do? said Kyle.

I know exactly what community means, said Mo.

On the shelf by the window there was a line of OPI nail varnishes, running the range of colours of the spectrum, twenty of them. Mo watched as he used the back of his little finger to push from the left so that the varnishes fell slowly on to the tiles, one at a time. All twenty bottles, one at a time.

Only two actually smashed, a coral and a hot red.

You need to watch it, he said.

Mo swallowed. That leather jacket would be wipe-clean.

It'll need to be in an envelope, Kyle said. And it'll be a Friday.

On his way out he turned around. And you'll also be giving me a Christmas and Easter extra. Plus something over the holiday.

I'm talking money, he said. Fuck sake don't flatter yourself love.

Hey, she shouted after him, when she knew he couldn't hear. Hey, big man! You left your ball!

Another late night it would have to be then. Nothing else for it. In the appointments book she ruled the line for Tuesday down to the bottom of the page.

Kyle

The cemetery sloped down the side of the hill. Although it was big, there was rarely anyone there during the week and it was always cold up there, looking over the city. The older graves had granite surrounds and marble chips, some kept white with squirts of bleach, but most were green and mildewed. Kyle was at the lower section, the newer space, where the graves were less grandiose – just headstones side by side. He was nervous walking towards it. Over the past year there'd been the time when it had been spray painted with red loops – you wouldn't have known what it said, if it said anything – and then there was the day when someone must have taken a sledgehammer to it. They'd knocked off a great lump. Scum, pure and simple. The worst time, and Jesus this was the worst time, was when somebody had shat on the side of the tombstone. They'd smeared it across his name, David Ian Starrs, and when Kyle saw it he was disgusted to the pit of his stomach. He had only been wearing a T-shirt and he took it off, run it under the tap at the bottom of the graveyard. He attacked the stone with a fury and thought about the sound of cracking bone and the way a lip swells.

T-shirt had been stinking. He couldn't see a bin so he just bunched it up and threw it a couple of rows away where it landed on an urn.

There's a fella's feeling the heat, said a fat man who was getting a bunch of flowers out of the back seat of his car.

What did you say? Kyle went over to him. What did you just say?

Nothing mate. The man held out his hands and shook his head. No offence. It was just, you know – and he pointed at Kyle's bare chest – feeling the heat.

Kyle grabbed the bunch of dog daisies and shoved them into the man's face, right into his mouth. He was making a choking sound and the flowers were falling apart but he still kept pushing.

Who the fuck do you think you are? Kyle said, genuinely inquisitive. Like who?

He didn't tell Grace about the man and the flowers but he told her what had happened to the grave this time.

Who's responsible for doing that? she had asked.

Don't know, he said, but he knew it could be several different people, several different groups. Davy's funeral had actually been on the TV, well the local news at six in the evening, but by the later news something else had replaced it. Afterwards they had sat in the bar with Davy's three little children marauding around and the two practically identical ex-partners. But today the grave was fine and nobody had touched it. Kyle traced the golden lettering with his finger.

Grace had said that they were going out for their dinner that night but he had not been enthusiastic. Well, we're going, she had said, and that's that.

Why? he had asked.

Just are. It's bring your own, so if you want to, bring your own. It's just new opened. I met the guy who runs it's wife.

Do we have to?

Yes.

Well, I got stuff to do. Tell me where it is and I'll just meet you there.

Kyle's stuff. A diverse portfolio. He had heard somebody say that once and he had liked it so he used it. Things had been better though: money came in well enough most of the time, but it wasn't always easy to maintain control. The taxi company, such as it was, did all right delivering the after-hours what have you, and then there was the shop and the mechanics that he had a main cut in. Most places were still paying up, as were the small dealers, but nothing felt secure. What was it? It was just – maybe it wasn't any different from what it had ever been and it was just him. Davy going had been terrible. That coroner: heart attack brought on by steroid abuse, no way was Kyle having that. Why wasn't everybody having heart attacks then if that was the case?

To All Their Dues

Basically the enemy was everywhere and there wasn't anybody left to trust except Grace who he did trust even though she probably disapproved of everything. Once, when there was a situation, she had been taken in for questioning for a day and a half and she had said nothing. In fact, one of them had said to him, you're punching above with that one Kyle. There were Hungarians on the scene now, they smashed up one of the bars and they were making inroads into things. And your woman, lippy fuck, going on about community the other day, oh I know about community, should've firebombed the place. Might still. The sort of people that were coming up now, they weren't the same. Boys were stupid, the ones who would have been part of it in the past now went to university, cleared out.

But maybe it was just him. That was why he was going to try this place, against his better judgement. A flyer had come through the door about it but it was far enough away for very few people to recognise him. It was above a dry cleaners. He'd been past the other day to see what it looked like, the Class A Hypnotherapy. Just a staircase up and then some net curtains. Looked a dump, but if it worked it worked. Nothing else – and he had tried a lot of stuff – had made any difference.

The waiting room was a small white cube and on the wall there were testimonials from people who had been successfully treated at Class A Hypnotherapy. There was some ponce who he had never heard of saying that Class A had cured him of his stage fright and that he was ready to do a summer season in Blackpool for the first time in years. Fella looked a fruit, him and his nerves. Fuck him and his nerves. And then there was some student who had written to say that her troubles had cleared up thanks to yeah yeah yeah. There was a candle oil burner and the place smelled of a plant and the music was like you'd get in a Chinese. Kyle lifted out the candle and burned along the edge of one of the brochures on the table, setting fire to an inch or so at a time, and then blowing it out. When he'd done around the whole brochure he blew out the candle.

He heard voices, somebody coming out of the room and going down the stairs, and then a man appeared in the waiting room. Geoff, he said, extending his hand. Very pleased to meet you.

Kyle stood up.

And you are, he got a diary out of his pocket, you are–

Marty, said Kyle.

Well, Marty, please come on through.

The Chinese music was still on the go in the other room and there was a beige sofa where Kyle was told to sit because there needed to be a consultation before any treatment could begin.

We need to fill in a questionnaire, said Geoff. Your other name, Marty?

Kyle thought for a minute. The only thing that came to mind was Pellow.

Pellow, he said.

Alright, said Geoff, as he filled the boxes. Marty Pellow.

Address?

Look no, said Kyle. Never mind my address. Are you gonna just get on with this?

I do need your GP's name, said Geoff with an apologetic smile. Who would your GP be now, Marty?

Arches, he said.

Right you are, said Geoff, writing in The Arches Medical Centre. So, he said, admin done, what brings you along to us today?

Kyle shrugged. Just the usual.

Geoff continued to look at him, his pen poised. Just what, Marty? How do you feel?

Alright.

You feel alright. What would alright be on a scale of 1 to 10?

Jeez. Seven out of ten, Kyle said. Maybe an eight. Now that, said Geoff, is really quite good.

Yeah, so? said Kyle.

If most days you feel seven, maybe an eight, then why, Marty, have you come to see us?

There's only you here, yeah? asked Kyle. Why you keep saying us? Why you keep saying that when it's only you?

People come to us for all sorts of reasons, Geoff continued. Some want to give up smoking say, others have a specific fear, of flying perhaps, or maybe they feel nervous thinking about a particular event.

Kyle's face showed his opinion of these kinds of people. And then there are those who come to us because they experience high levels of anxiety, manifest quite possibly in panic attacks, sleeplessness, or obsessive-compulsive disorders–

Alright, said Kyle, don't be telling me any more about these people, I don't care. Could we just get on with whatever it is you do like, you know, maybe now. If that's convenient.

Geoff indicated a chair over in the corner. You sure you want to continue, Marty? he said. There's not a lot of point in continuing if you feel this isn't for you. The will must be there.

Well, he wasn't expecting it to be a man swinging a watch on a chain and saying look into my eyes but this was just a chair with your man perched on the desk, but then the chair reclined, like a La-Z-Boy, but so far back it wasn't a telly you were watching, it was the ceiling. There was a black spot on the ceiling. The man had gone out and come back with a blanket and a cushion that had been heated up.

Kyle threw the cushion on the floor. I don't think we'll be needing that, mate. He kicked off the blanket. All this shit would you just make a start here?

Geoff started to say the spiel. He was reading it off, you could tell, the way he was savouring every word. Something about a beach and the sun shining: yeah, he could imagine the beach, he could imagine a few hot birds in bikinis, okay well now they were starting to get off with each other. Well, that was pretty all right to think about, but Geoff said *Focus* really loud and then he was back to the room, listening to that voice of his going on about different parts of the body. That Chinese music was still on the go, the ribs and the black bean sauce, wee doll bringing over a sizzling dish, you spinning that revolving table. Mandarin City. Cueball ate the fortune cookie at the end, bit of paper and all. How the fuck was I meant to know, he said, give me yours and I'll eat it as well. That was a while ago though, some laugh, that fella was long gone.

Geoff was saying to think about contentment, when you felt in control, and Kyle is in the old front room where their dad is lying half on, half off the rug and the blood from his mouth is pooling on the floor. A couple of weeks before Davy had asked, you know the way I'm fourteen and you know the way you're thirteen? You put us together do we equal a man of twenty-seven? Must have put it into their heads they could swing it – and they did because when the old fella hit Davy full on the face the two of them laid into him and there he was on the floor. Still dangerous because they couldn't afford for him to get either one of them alone, but even that would only be for a certain period of time because they were getting stronger and his boozing was getting worse. Pathetic him lying there. Felt good to see the legs collapse from under him, pathetic the way he tried to appeal to them through the blood. Davy! And then, Kyle!

Even their ma was pleased. She said oh what's the world coming to, and all of that stuff, but she was happy and they knew it. She put a tea towel over his head. And that was what Kyle was thinking of, that was a good day.

Try to take a snapshot of that contentment, focus on a detail of that scene if you can, said Geoff, are you focusing Marty, on something specific? (Yes: the blood on the floor way darker than you'd think.) Can you do that, Marty? That's good. Good. You are going to hold that in your mind as a motif of happiness that you can refer to. You holding it in your mind?

I am, said Kyle.

And how are you feeling? asked Geoff.

Okay.

You're feeling good? asked Geoff.

Okay, said Kyle.

Hold that image and know that you are the same person who can achieve that contentment again, whenever you want, Marty.

But no, Kyle thought. No. Because Davy wasn't here and that made everything not the same. What the fuck was he doing lying with a blanket round him on a chair above the dry cleaners listening to this pure shite, how bad had things got that this was what he was at?

Right, that's it. Over, that's enough. Will you move this fucking – he tried to push himself out of the chair – this fucking–

Geoff spoke calmly. The initial session can sometimes be a little underwhelming. Next time–

There'll be no next time, said Kyle. That's it.

Geoff took an invoice from a pad at the desk, calmly filled it in, and handed it to Kyle.

You got to be having a laugh, he said. Eighty quid to lie back in a chair and listen to you reading a script off a page, well I do not think so. Here, he hoked around in the pocket of his jacket, that'll do you, and he handed him a fiver. You are making easy money, pal, let me tell you with this fucking caper.

Geoff watched from the window as Kyle got into his car, slammed the door shut.

Kyle Starrs, he said aloud.

The restaurant had had a refit since it had been the burger bar. There were now white tiles and pictures from local artists. Every table had a couple of tea lights and a posy in a jam jar. Grace was already there, sitting at the table. Kyle came in, clinking with bottles.

Can I take those for you? the fella asked.

Kyle lifted out two bottles of Moët, and a bottle of Courvoisier.

One of those over in an ice bucket, he said. What? he said to Grace.

Nothing.

It's bring your own, yeah?

It's bring your own.

Well, then. What's the issue?

She sighed. Doesn't matter.

It's bring your own and I've brought my own. Jesus Christ.

The young man brought over the menus.

I'm actually quite hungry, Grace said. Haven't eaten anything all day.

Well, order whatever you want. Here, what's the hold-up with the drink? Kyle said. Oi! Mate! He pointed to the table. Drink?

The fella came over, apologetic. It's just that, we don't have any ice buckets yet. We're only open, I mean, we're only just open so not everything's quite right yet.

Grace smiled at him. No problem, she said.

Hick joint, said Kyle when the waiter had gone. Don't think much of this place.

Wise up, Kyle, Grace said. Just leave it for goodness sake.

The fella came back with the champagne, glasses and an improvised ice bucket in the form of a vase. Oh, not for me, Grace said when, having filled Kyle's, the waiter went to pour her a glass. I'm happy with this. She pointed to her tonic water.

Right you are, he said.

When the fella moved to the next table, Kyle poured Grace a glass of champagne. Cheers, he said.

I don't want any, Kyle. I said to you.

God, a glass won't kill you.

I don't want it.

There was no enjoyment in drinking by yourself. That voice of hers killed him. Always calm. He once had said to her, you know who you remind me of? Clint Eastwood.

That's flattering, she said.

I know it is, he had replied.

But she could make you feel like nothing. She wasn't impressed by much: a five star would mean as much as a two star. Jewellery she wasn't into. Not interested in fancy places, well that was obvious when you took a look around here. They could have been in the town at somewhere where you got treated really well, where there were plenty of people about to see you out and about. He knew fine rightly that she knew about the various other women over the years, but she never made a scene. He wouldn't have minded her being bothered, full-on furious, he wouldn't have minded if she'd punched and slapped him. Even that one time when your woman that he had seen on and off for a few months came around to the house to make a row, she had just said, a friend of yours to see you, and gone out of the house. Did your woman ever regret that one, but Grace never mentioned it again other than to say, please try to avoid that kind of thing, Kyle, because I could do without it. The young fella was over asking them if they had decided what they wanted. Grace said she would have the pulled pork and Kyle said he wanted the steak. He hadn't looked at the menu, but he wanted the steak.

Well done, he said. I like it, you know, really well done.

The fella went away and then came back. It's just, he said, it's just that the chef says that it's a minute steak.

So what? Kyle said.

Minute steaks are meant to be cooked quickly. That's what the chef says, he added carefully.

No, said Kyle. Well cooked. End of.

Grace leaned across the table. They're only saying that if you want it well done, it's likely to be tough because minute steaks need to be fried quick.

Did we come out for a cookery lesson? Did we? Minute steak. What a load of shite.

The woman appeared at the table. We're sorry about the steak situation, she said. Maybe there's something else on the menu that you would like to choose.

No love, said Kyle. I've made my order, thank you very much.

Were you busy today? Grace asked.

Kyle shrugged. Just the usual. Was up at the grave, he said.

Used to be small, that graveyard, said Grace. It's eaten up most of that hill now. Everybody all together in that graveyard, she said.

Yeah well, said Kyle. Death comes to us all. Grim Reaper. Does that steak come with sauce? Can't remember, he said. I don't want the sauce all over the top of it. I hate when they do that, slather the sauce all over the top of it.

The young fella came over to top up Kyle's glass of champagne.

You celebrating something? he asked.

No, said Kyle. That guy's doing my head in, he said to Grace when he had gone.

He's just doing his job Kyle, she said.

The steak, when it arrived, was a pathetic specimen, a shrivelled offering.

Well you got what you asked for, said Grace. You can't complain. So don't complain.

Kyle tried to cut it but it didn't yield.

Fucking shoe leather, he said. That's gonna bounce off the walls.

Try some of this, said Grace. It's nice. We'll share it and they can bring us another plate.

So I've come out for half a meal, he thought. I can't even get a proper meal. That ponce, what had he said to think about, what did he tell me, and he thought, yes, it was his da lying half on half off the rug. Davy had wanted to wrap that electric flex around his neck, the one that he used to hit them, but he had said no just leave it, that was enough, enough for now. Sore being hit with that flex.

Grace

The worst was the street-preaching when they stood in Cornmarket on a Saturday afternoon with two speakers, a microphone and a cardboard box full of tracts. If it rained they put the box in a black bin bag. On the rare occasion they went to places like Portadown or Lurgan and Grace didn't mind this so much because there would be no chance of seeing anyone from school. It would be the usual: you'd be cold and you'd get people either shouting abuse or laughing at you, but at least no one would know who you were.

There were things you could do to pass the time. You could count the paving stones for as far as they stretched into the distance; they started square and then, as they got further and further away, became wafers. You could hold your breath until you saw someone with a pink coat. Then you could hold your breath until you saw someone with a green coat. Then you could hold your breath until you saw someone in brown boots. You could do those same things in Cornmarket but you had no anonymity. Three o'clock on a Saturday afternoon there would be all the shrieking laughing crowd from school. Is that not your wee woman from our year? Your wee doll in that big coat? It is her. Feel wick for her. Shout something over but.

Sometimes there would be competition from other groups: fire-eaters, choirs and, now and again, breakdancers who would bring a CD player and turn it up loud until the sound broke. Grace's dad would turn up the preacher's volume and his sound won out because it had an amp. It was a cosmic battle between good and evil right there in Cornmarket, transmogrified into a street sermon versus 2 Unlimited.

An American evangelist had held an old-time crusade in a huge white tent on the O'Neill Road and the very first night he went Grace's dad had some kind of epiphany. On the next evening Grace's mum had one too. They started going to a mission hall that was opposite an old dairy and constructed out of corrugated iron. Women had to wear hats. There were some people who had apparently been very bad like Jimmy Baker who had given his testimony and told everyone about how he had found the Lord after being a gambler and a womaniser and a communist street fighter. Jimmy Baker seemed so nice, sucking his mints in the back row.

Sunday clothes were uncomfortable in ways you could not have imagined. The tights were always too small and the good wool skirt scratched. The label on the nape of the jacket was stiff but it was stitched right in so you couldn't cut it out. The hat was like a pancake. There were lots of ways you could wear a beret, Grace's mother had said. Yeah and every one of them stupid. The shop windows showed bright clothes, tight clothes. You walked past people, women, and they were all like the drawings in the maths book with the compass, soft concurrent semicircles. Grace's clothes, bought at charity shops, were chosen for their amorphous quality. Her mother talked about 'good' materials, wools, gabardine, camel hair, durable and decent. The girls in her class used tampons. Grace's mother thought tampons tantamount to rape.

The preacher was called the Reverend Dr Emery. Everything he said was in groups of three. Sin, despair and iniquity. Our Saviour past present and future. A strong, hot, welcome cup of tea, available at the back of the church after the service. The long, boring, repetitive service. You could stare at the Reverend Dr Emery in the pulpit until he doubled and became surrounded in black light and then you could look at the ceiling and see his outline in relief against the whitewashed beams. You could make bargains with the Lord. I will believe if you make your woman there's hat fall off. She scratches her neck. Split second when you think it might happen. Hat stays on. You could listen to tales from a mostly Old Testament world of hard justice. You could listen to his lamenting tone: oh why is the world filled with such evil? You could think: I don't know if I believe this.

Then the Carson family started coming. They were tall, thin people, a husband and wife, who had been in Malawi for many years, mostly working on bible translation but involved in other projects too. Their own children had long left home but they fostered kids, short term, and they had plenty of room in their big double-fronted house with the overgrown garden. First there was a boy, about ten, who had a hearing aid and a green coat. Grace wondered if he could hear what the Reverend Dr Emery said; he mouthed the hymns like he was dubbed. Then there was an older boy, although he wasn't there for that long, whose head was always cocked to one side; oh aye right, it said. Then there was a girl who overlapped with him for a month or so, fat with a pale face. Grace's mother had said, why don't you go over and talk to her after church, so Grace had tried but the girl hadn't asked her anything back. Grace shifted from foot to foot until it was time to go. And then there was the next one who had a clump of hair dyed pink. After one of the bible readings she shouted out, Amen! and then started laughing. There was embarrassed, irritated shooshing. Later, Grace's mum said, I think that girl's a bit lacking. Shouting out like that. People don't shout out like that in our church.

She did it with an American accent, said Grace.

She's a bit lacking.

But that didn't stop Grace's mother asking her to go around to help the girl, Kerri, with her schoolwork.

Why? said Grace. It didn't go well, speaking to the other one.

This is a different girl. She needs help with her schoolwork.

Why can't Mrs Carson help her?

She's busy. You're going round tonight. I said to them that you would.

Like I'm the genius.

Don't be cheeky, Grace, her mother had said.

Mrs Carson said the bedroom was the first door on the right at the top of the stairs. Should she knock? Grace wasn't sure.

Hello, she called.

What you want? the girl Kerri said from inside. And then she came to the door. What you want?

I'm meant to help you with stuff, said Grace. That's what they said for me to come and do.

Who?

Them.

What stuff?

School stuff.

I don't go to school, Kerri said.

Then why did they send me?

I go to a centre.

They said I was to help you.

Well, I don't want any help, Kerri said and closed the door.

But her mother sent her back again the next night. Sometimes it's necessary to persevere. We need to do what we can where we can.

Not you again, Kerri said, opening her door when Grace knocked. Behind her everything was around the bed like a magnet: clothes, magazines, dirty tights with the knickers still in them, cans of coke. You could smell body spray but mainly smoke. Did the Carsons not notice?

Did you not get the message last time? she said. Why you here again?

Mrs Carson called them downstairs. Kerri screwed up her face. On the dining-room table there was a book with a rabbit on the front cover and a worksheet. The other kids were playing out in the garden, even though it was raining a bit. Mrs Carson said, Kerri, I want you to remember the talk we had earlier. You remember? No effort made with work, no allowance. No allowance, no whatever it is you like to buy.

Kerri scowled across the table at Grace. Then she lifted the book about the rabbit and opened it at a random page. Her finger slowly ran under each word and her lips silently formed the words. She read about ten pages like this, with Grace looking on redundant.

Then she sighed, closed the book. Done, she said.

What's it about? asked Grace.

Fucking rabbit, said Kerri. Did you not see the front of it?

Is that what you have to read?

If it wasn't, you think I'd be looking at it huh?

It's a rabbit that goes around doing stuff, she added.

She dropped the book on the floor.

The other one was about a homeless man, she said.

Was it better? Grace asked.

No, said Kerri.

Come on up the stairs, she said. I want to show you something.

Grace thought that Mrs Carson might object but she was involved in doing something in the kitchen and so said nothing. Grace found herself sitting on Kerri's rumpled bed. Kerri was pulling something out from behind her wardrobe. She sat down on the bed beside Grace with a magazine.

Never mind that, look at this, she said.

She opened the magazine at a page where there was a woman lying on a sofa with her legs wide open. Not totally naked: she had on gold platform heels.

What do you think of that then? said Kerri, holding it up close to Grace's face.

Grace said nothing.

What do you think of that?

She turned to another page with two women.

And that?

To All Their Dues

Never you mind you coming round here to tell me about this that or yon, you don't know it all. Look at it again. Look at this one. They're all at it. All that lot in that tin box just the same as everyone else.

You're not normal, Kerri went on. You're really weird. I seen you sitting there with those two, your mum and dad, all holy holy, and I think, God help you. You know Helen Watson who used to live here, well she said the same thing about you. Said you were a psycho.

You're the one who's not normal, said Grace.

Oh aye is that right? I'm not going round like a granny mush fucking mouse. What you frightened of? Burning in hell?

No, said Grace. I'm not going to burn in hell.

Here let me tell you something, said Kerri. Let me tell you something. What year were you born in? What year was it?

1980, said Grace.

1980. So in 1979 you weren't here. Were you bothered? You weren't. So when you're not here again because you're dead, will you be bothered? No. You weren't before – so you won't be again.

Grace thought about this.

Hah! said Kerri. Think about that one. Put that in your pipe and smoke it. Aw, but no, you can't because Jesus says don't smoke.

1979. It was a nothing.

Kerri started reading the description of the woman from the magazine. Here listen, she said. Listen to this. She read it with a big pause between each word, the cadence of a kid, following the line with her finger. Cindy... likes... Cindy likes–

What? said Grace. What is it Cindy likes?

Kerri puzzled at the word.

Maybe, said Grace, maybe you should stick to the rabbit book, Kerri.

Kerri rolled up the mag and threw it at Grace. Read it yourself, she said.

Grace grabbed it, twisted it tight and hit Kerri across the cheek with it.

I didn't want to come here. Do you understand that?

Kerri came charging across the room, grabbed Grace by the hair and threw her onto the bed, elbowed her hard in the gut. Grace gasped – she couldn't breathe out. But it was easier to hit Kerri than she would have thought; her fist made contact with her stomach, taut as a drum, and she hit her again and again. They fell onto the floor on top of the dirty tights and the dirty plates. Kerri was quick and heavy, the ways she flipped Grace over, twisting her arm up behind her back. She couldn't move and Kerri kept pushing harder so that she thought she was going to be sick. And then Kerri stopped. She was panting, trying to catch her breath. All Grace could smell was fags and hot fabric conditioner. Mrs Carson must put loads in the washes. Kerri took another handful of her hair and Grace thought she was going to get hit again but instead Kerri's mouth was soft although you could taste the blood like a coin.

At home Grace's mother was sewing a hem.

All go well? she asked.

It was alright, Grace said.

There are some booklets you could take round next time. There's those new ones that were sent from the States.

Sure, said Grace.

Her mother's hand stretched the thread taut, did a final double stitch and cut the thread.

When they were next in church there was a big empty space at the end of the pew where the Carsons sat. Kerri wasn't there. It was the same the week after and the week after that. After church Mrs Carson said that she was grateful that Grace had helped Kerri along a bit, but that she had gone back to live with her mother now. They come and they go, Mrs Carson said. This is for you, she said. She gave Grace a folded up piece of paper with an address and phone number on it. The frill of a spiral bound page torn off. Big bubble writing: written with careful deliberation, nearly pressed through the page. She kept the paper even though she knew that she was never going to phone or call round. She couldn't imagine it: going to the pictures with Kerri; going for a meal with Kerri. Sending each other a Valentine: it seemed preposterous.

The next week Grace didn't go to church. She said it was because she wasn't well, but when her mother came up to her room, she said the thing is I'm giving going to church a miss for the time being. She knew that they prayed for her all the time. They sent Reverend Dr Emery around to see her and she sipped a cup of tea slowly while he told her about lost sheep and the prodigal son. He tried to scare her by talking about girls he had heard of who had strayed from the righteous path and who, without exception, had come to a bad end. They would congregate at the front door, there would be whispering and then he would go. There would invariably be a quiet knock on her door. Everything alright, Grace? Her mother would be hopeful. Fine, Grace would nod.

There was pain and there was passion and there was no God. Some people had to wait a lifetime to find out that kind of thing, had to study and read books, gaze up at the stars. But it had been made apparent to her when she was young, it had come all in a rush when someone was whacking her with a porno mag. You might never experience that intensity of revelation ever, ever again.

You lived your life. You didn't expect anything too much. There were holidays and meals and trips to the multiplex and city breaks. There was work in the nursery, which was good fun most of the time. All that intensity was a long time ago now. She loved Kyle and wouldn't leave him. Would he have been like how he was if it hadn't been for that brother of his, getting him into stuff? Good riddance to Davy. Live by the sword die by the sword. Matthew 26:52. She could remember that. Grace had found out she couldn't have kids. They had tried IVF but it hadn't worked. She had been frightened he would go off with one of the others but he didn't. Doesn't matter, he said. I've got you and that's what matters. Sex was useless because she felt a dud.

She went to church one time, nostalgic for her youth, when she saw a poster for a crusade, but it was a small scale affair that took place in a hall where the floor was marked out for badminton and basketball with coloured tape. All the people were old and had all been saved years ago. There was no singing, only a man and a

PowerPoint, but she ended up helping out with the teas because there was something wrong with the urn.

This morning Grace was leaving stuff at the dry cleaners and then going to the beauty place. She had been there practically every other week since it opened. She had never thought before that she was high maintenance, but now it turned out that she was. She wouldn't have thought of going there if she hadn't seen the advert and the voucher in the paper. The woman was just starting out. Weird little box of a place but she liked it. It was always warm, and it smelled of coconut. The girl didn't say much which was good. The first time she had gone, it had been for a leg wax. It was sore. The woman had said, next time, take a couple of paracetamol before you come. You know what in fact, she had said, take a couple of paracetamol and a brandy. Can only make it better. She had taken neither the paracetamol nor the brandy. The girl's face was sometimes only a couple of inches away from you: you could run your finger along that frown of concentration. That ponytail, you could wrap it round and round your fist, pull it tight. She always looked preoccupied. Grace thought about her all the time. What did other people think of? Lying on beaches? Being in the Caribbean? To do lists? Grace thought about the taste of blood, a woman in gold high heels, lying face down on a bed. It was a disappointment every time when the woman said, well that's it, I'll leave you to get ready and I'll see you outside. The dull thud of the well this is all there is.

And here she was again, back for more, sitting waiting for the woman to get the room ready. She looked at the line of moisturisers, the row of nail varnishes, the stack of magazines.

What happened the window? Grace asked when the girl appeared.

It'll be fixed this morning, she said, if the fella ever arrives. Go on into the room, it's all set up, and I'll be through in a minute.

Giving Just Enough

Wendy Erskine on To All Their Dues

Wendy Erskine's first collection of stories, Sweet Home, *was shortlisted for the Edge Hill Prize and the Republic of Consciousness Prize and won the 2020 Butler Literary Prize. Her second collection,* Dance Move, *was published earlier in 2022. She works as a school teacher in Belfast.*

'To All Their Dues' was her first story to be published – I wanted to know how in this early story, and in all her work, she was able to orchestrate vivid characters within such rich stories.

What was your starting point for this story? When did you realise it was in three sections?

I knew I wanted to write a story that was in some way set in a beauty salon; I liked the idea that it would be an absolute fast track to intimacy, that I could show people who in some ways might be very distant and yet in other ways were physically very close. That was the impetus for it.

But then I realised I was just as interested in the person who ran the beauty salon as the clients, which quickly became the idea of the three different voices.

It's very rarely that I have a structure before I begin. Normally, I want the characters to drive the story so that in a sense the events are revealed to me by the characters. To do this, I always write a very vague first draft and let the characters take it wherever they wish.

This was an unusual one because right from the beginning I wanted to include the three perspectives. It was also for me quite schematic that I wanted to have repetitions of threes – for example, the first line of the story references a triple, and later on there's a minister with a tripartite sermon structure: there's threes the whole way through it.

You say your stories are character-driven, and yet your sentences are so adept at furthering the plot; I wondered how you came to marry the both so well? Is that in the editing?

Yes, I suppose no one in life thinks they are a minor character. What I'm trying to do as much as possible is to get complexity in at every turn, so I write a very long first draft – maybe three times what I need – so when I am putting the story together, there is a complexity to even a very minor character, because they'd had perhaps 3 or 4,000 words devoted to them in an earlier incarnation of the story.

That thing that is often said about the short story form that every single sentence must drive the story forward – I've got to say I don't entirely agree with it. In, say, a story that's 5,000 words long, there's also the room for aspects of the story that are providing a kind of complexity or nuance or supplying a kind of a texture. For example, in this story, there would be Mo's previous working experience on the fortune telling line. Strictly speaking, if someone asked: 'how is that advancing the plot of the story, how is that moving the story in a particular way?' I'd say: 'it's not – what it's doing is providing a kind of complexity to this particular character.'

Also, I absolutely hate the idea of backstory. I think that's such a misnomer. It gives the impression that the past is always subservient to the present and that people's past experiences are only interesting and have validity in how they form the present. I don't really like that; to me all these things are written concurrently.

How I decide what to keep in and what to take out – because you don't want it just to be an accretion of random details about people that go on for thousands of words – it's just working out what it is that gives the reader *enough* to be able to form a judgement about the character in a situation.

The narrator's voice feels very personable, almost chatty – not always strictly grammatically correct – and as a result very present. How did you come to this voice?

It's very rarely that I'm moving out of third person. I find close third person incredibly flexible as it offers me every advantage of first person's interiority and flow, plus you can move to being slightly distant from the character. However, that can sometimes pose a problem as, if you make the third person too distant, it then skews how the characters are being presented. So what I try to do is, even in third person narration without the thoughts or the interiority, is use vocabulary or expressions that in some ways reflect that character. For example, with Grace, I'll use a word like 'transmogrify.' Grace doesn't say that in her dialogue – that's the third person narrator saying it – but I wouldn't use that word with Kyle or Mo just because, even in the third person narration which is not necessarily a presentation of their thoughts, it just isn't going to fit.

Could you say more about what relationship this narration has to the character? For example, is it in some way a reflection of the character?

The narration stands not necessarily as a reflection of their value system or beliefs – it's quite often a reasonably objective third person narration. Although it is not one that's massively at odds with the character in terms of language and style.

I always found this interesting, how to write the third person aspect that's not the actual character. To write in a way that suits the character also means not trying to be really clever and really meretricious in terms of style or language. So sometimes it could be chatty, as you said, if that particular character demands that style of narration.

What's more, if I did write about Kyle in a very lofty third person narration which offers some kind of authorial comment, it would then distance him as a person and probably strip him of some level of humanity – even though he's a dreadful character – and I'm not really into doing that.

How important is humour to your telling of this story? For example, was it an important part of your description of Grace's key turning point: 'it had all come in a rush when someone was whacking her with a porno mag'?

A lot of the time this is not particularly a conscious decision. It's not me thinking: *let's go for a really bathetic effect here – to go from something significant to something so trivial is going to be funny here.* I just think it is my sensibility: no matter what you give me, no matter whatever locale or characters, I'm going to still write in that kind of way – joy and woe, that sort of thing. I think that's all you've got as a writer. There's a Zola quote that 'art is a corner of creation seen through a temperament', and my temperament is going to be seeing serious things and funny things absolutely coexisting. That's what I do and you can take it or leave it.

Mo's section starts with her surrendering her once-held ideas about making her salon a Caribbean paradise, which mirrors her finally resigning herself to Kyle's extortion. Is this surrender a tragedy and the victory of hatred? Or, is it an important step for her to make compromises in order to live alongside people?

I think it's the latter. She starts with a vision for her domain and very quickly sees it can't be maintained because of circumstances. I never really thought of it before as a miniature of what happens later in the way she has to acquiesce to Kyle.

What I'm looking at is the whole idea of compromise and the idea that all the characters might have an ideal version of how life should be that is so dependent on circumstances beyond their control, and so their reality ends up quite far from where they'd like it to be. There isn't even a distress about it, just a weary acknowledgment that that is how life works out.

It's a simplistic question but is this something like a moral to the story?

I don't know if it's a moral in the sense that I'm presenting it in some kind of didactic purpose that people need to learn a lesson through this about how life operates, but it's certainly a reflection or a take on how life often is.

I loved the line of Mo's, when Kyle smashes the bottles and she thinks: 'That leather jacket would be wipe-clean.' Do you remember how a line like this came into the story?

I do remember it really really clearly. I was once in a cafe, not a beauty salon, and I remember this guy in a leather jacket came into the cafe to collect protection money. I can remember the way he walked which was simultaneously jaunty and menacing. I can remember just noticing the way he walked and what he was wearing and I suppose the whole idea of leather.

In totally different circumstances, when I had my two kids I was wearing leather all the time because it was wipe-clean, it just seemed incredibly practical. So in some ways I wanted it to be both practical and slightly sinister that she imagines that if he gets blood on the jacket or is in any way sullied by conflict he can just wipe it off. While she gets stuck with the smashed bottles.

It reminds me of what you said earlier about making characters complex. Though sentences like this don't further the plot obviously, this extra detail enriches the story.

Yes, with a character like Kyle it might be easy to see him as two-dimensional, throwing his weight around but the more you can present him as a complex character – someone who is dreadful though in other ways ridiculous – the better reading experience it is.

The story of Mo's coming to terms with intimidation starts subtly from the brevity of the butcher's sympathy and the 'old fella' shrugging, and builds from there. Did you plan for this escalation, find it happening as you wrote, or add it after writing your initial draft?

I don't really know what's happening initially, in the sense that I have a rough idea of where things are going to go, but I'm always prepared to be surprised – and I'm actually delighted when I am surprised by how things turn out. I write that first draft with very few restrictions and just take it in whatever way it goes.

I knew at the beginning Mo was going to be very startled by what happens. I reckoned that to make it reasonably realistic, other people on the road would be already paying this protection money so I knew there wasn't going to be a band of people who had organised themselves to combat people like Kyle. I knew she would get a level of support but no more than a few words and maybe lending her something to patch up the window. Then, as I was writing it, I wondered how far she was going to go in terms of standing up to him. That was where she does actually push it and gives the implication that her definition of community is very different to his definition of community and how it operates.

So I suppose, even in that first draft, when I was writing it, I did want the tension to be quite incremental and then deflated at the end when she decides she's just going to go along with it.

When the story lingers on the first eyebrow wax of the day or Mo's previous job in the call centre, what criteria do you have for what stays and what goes when you're 'putting the story together'?

When I'm editing my very long first draft, I'll read it back, thinking to myself, *what is this story?* It's not about what am I keeping and what am I jettisoning, it's actually me asking what *is* the story here? Because sometimes things that I thought in the first draft were of consequence, I read back and realise they're utterly inconsequential, and that things that are peripheral are actually things where there's complexity and interest.

Giving Just Enough

It's the most important process for me in the writing and all I can say is it's kind of a *feel*; a feel for giving the reader just enough for them to put their own ideas into the story and meet me halfway. And it often involves me cutting out things that I think are good or funny or clever. And so, to be honest, one of the areas I want to cut away is where I feel I am present, where I think I'm making myself look smart. Which I know is contradictory in a sense because with a story I'm saying 'this is all my sensibility, this is all me and my take on the world', but what I don't want to have are bits that are self-consciously *me* trying to be clever.

I also often cut away a lot of physical description because in a sense I think it's more satisfying for a reader to have to invest that aspect themselves in a story.

Encouraging a reader to invest in the story, is that effect created from the questions that you leave unanswered, like what will happen after each tale, or what are the characters truly like? How do you write a story that is so alive with ambiguity?

Being alive with ambiguity: that's the highest praise. For me it is really really important that the story exists beyond the end of the piece, that the reader has a projected idea of what's going to occur in future time.

Is this ambiguity what you meant earlier about something being 'enough' for a reader?

Yes, I want that idea of tolerance of ambiguity. Some people like things to be fairly cut and dried and can find my short stories very unresolved with the endings I write. They may say 'what was the point of that or what was all that about, I couldn't understand the ending.'

I suppose a lot of the time, I'm trying to think: *can the reader tolerate all these levels of ambiguity in why people do the things they do.* And there are some points where I think to myself: *no, that's a step too far,* and I'll need to take it back a little bit. Say, for example, why is somebody like Grace with Kyle? In some ways it's not clear, but in other ways I went quite far along the line of showing they love each other – I think it's reasonably explicit. It needed to be done just to secure that for people, so they didn't feel these two entirely different people are utterly mismatched. I'm relying on someone understanding Kyle's character enough to know that telling your wife she reminds you of Clint Eastwood is something very flattering as far as he is concerned.

You said this was the third story of yours to be published. Can you think of ways it was a development on from your earlier writing?

It was a very long story, I think at that point the longest story that The Stinging Fly had ever published. So there was a level of complexity in it that would have been greater than my earlier stories, simply because they were shorter.

My two earlier stories – 'Locksmiths' and 'The soul has no skin' which both ended up in *Sweet Home* – are also stories that are complicated in terms of how time is manipulated, moving between three or four timelines. Although definitely this was the one it was just the most complex in its different voices and perspectives.

And what do you like in the story, reading it again now?

One of my favourite things I've ever written is the description of self-harm being like After Eights. I don't really think I've written much else that's surpassed that. I'm very pleased with that little simile.

Would you do anything differently now?

There are some things that I would do differently now. There's things I do in this that I wouldn't do now, and I wonder if I *should* do them now. I don't regard them necessarily as rookie things.

I wonder also if I would call it 'To All Our Dues.' Originally, the title of the story was 'Triptych' which became 'To All Our Dues' for a more biblical resonance as it comes from 'Romans' – I don't know if 'Triptych' would have been a more straightforward title.

The repetition of threes I wouldn't do now as I think it is too schematic, too showy. Also that free-flowing thing where I've got Mo reminiscing about her previous job; even though I say not everything needs to drive the story forward, in this story I have just rolled with it and so there's whole sections there that are like vignettes or set pieces within the whole. I don't know if I would do that now – I think I would be much more disciplined.

Acknowledgements

'Maintenance' by Sussie Anie, first published in The White Review © 2020, used by permission of Mushens Entertainment Ltd.

'Path Lights' by Tom Drury. Copyright © Tom Drury, 2005. First published in The New Yorker, used by permission of The Wylie Agency (UK) Limited.

'To All Their Dues' by Wendy Erskine taken from *Sweet Home* © 2018, used by permission of Picador (Worldwide) and © 2016, used by permission of Stinging Fly Press (Republic of Ireland and Northern Ireland).

'Bad Dreams' from *Bad Dreams and Other Stories* by Tessa Hadley, published by Jonathan Cape. The story 'Bad Dreams' first appeared in the New Yorker. Reprinted by permission of Penguin Books Limited (Worldwide) and from *Bad Dreams and Other Stories* by Tessa Hadley. Copyright © 2017 by Tessa Hadley. Used by permission of HarperCollins Publishers (USA and Philippines).

'All Will Be Well' by Yiyun Li. Copyright © 2019, Yiyun Li, used by permission of The Wylie Agency (UK) Ltd.

'Ancient Ties of Karma' by Ben Okri. Copyright © Ben Okri 2020. Reproduced by permission of Ben Okri c/o Georgina Capel Associates Ltd., 29 Wardour Street, London, W1D 6PS.

'Bulk' was published in the collection 'Attrib. and other stories' by Eley Williams, published by Influx Press in 2017. Copyright © 2017 by Eley Williams.

This project has been made possible through the kind support of Cathy Galvin, founder and director of The Word Factory UK.

The *Reverse Engineering* series would not have been possible without the patience and diligence of Sally Thomas and Jessica Sanchez.